LITTLE CLASSICS

EDITED BY

ROSSITER JOHNSON

STORIES OF FORTUNE

BOSTON AND NEW YORK

HOUGHTON MIFFLIN COMPANY

The Riverside Press Cambridge

1914

CONTENTS.

THE GOLD-BUG.

BY EDGAR ALLAN POE.

MANY years ago I contracted an intimacy with a
Mr. William Legrand. He was of an ancient
Huguenot family, and had once been wealthy;
but a series of misfortunes had reduced him to want.
To avoid the mortification consequent upon his disasters,
he left New Orleans, the city of his forefathers, and
took up his residence at Sullivan's Island, near Charleston, South Carolina.

This island is a very singular one. It consists of
little else than the sea-sand, and is about three miles
long. Its breadth at no point exceeds a quarter of a
mile. It is separated from the mainland by a scarcely
perceptible creek oozing its way through a wilderness of
reeds and slime, a favorite resort of the marsh-hen. The
vegetation, as might be supposed, is scant, or at least
dwarfish. No trees of any magnitude are to be seen.
Near the western extremity, where Fort Moultrie stands,
and where are some miserable frame buildings, tenanted,

during summer, by the fugitives from Charleston dust
and fever, may be found, indeed, the bristly palmetto;
but the whole island, with the exception of this western
point, and a line of hard, white beach on the sea-coast,
is covered with a dense undergrowth of the sweet myrtle,
so much prized by the horticulturists of England. The
shrub here often attains the height of fifteen or twenty
feet, and forms an almost impenetrable coppice, burden-
ing the air with its fragrance.

In the inmost recesses of this coppice, not far from
the eastern or more remote end of the island, Legrand
had built himself a small hut, which he occupied when
I first, by mere accident, made his acquaintance. This
soon ripened into friendship, — for there was much in
the recluse to excite interest and esteem. I found him
well educated, with unusual powers of mind, but infected with misanthropy, and subject to perverse moods
of alternate enthusiasm and melancholy. He had with
him many books, but rarely employed them. His chief
amusements were gunning and fishing, or sauntering
along the beach and through the myrtles, in quest of
shells or entomological specimens; — his collection of
the latter might have been envied by a Swammer-
dam. In these excursions he was usually accompanied
by an old negro, called Jupiter, who had been manu-
mitted before the reverses of the family, but who could
be induced, neither by threats nor by promises, to aban-
don what he considered his right of attendance upon the
footsteps of his young "Massa Will." It is not improbable that the relatives of Legrand, conceiving him to be
somewhat unsettled in intellect, had contrived to instil

this obstinacy into Jupiter, with a view to the supervision and guardianship of the wanderer.

The winters in the latitude of Sullivan's Island are seldom very severe, and in the fall of the year it is a rare event indeed when a fire is considered necessary. About the middle of October, 18—, there occurred, however, a day of remarkable chilliness. Just before sunset I scrambled my way through the evergreens to the hut of my friend, whom I had not visited for several weeks, — my residence being, at that time, in Charleston, a distance of nine miles from the island, while the facilities of passage and re-passage were very far behind those of the present day. Upon reaching the hut I rapped, as was my custom, and getting no reply, sought for the key where I knew it was secreted, unlocked the door, and went in. A fine fire was blazing upon the hearth. It was a novelty, and by no means an ungrateful one. I threw off an overcoat, took an arm-chair by the crackling logs, and awaited patiently the arrival of my hosts.

Soon after dark they arrived, and gave me a most cordial welcome. Jupiter, grinning from ear to ear, bustled about to prepare some marsh-hens for supper. Legrand was in one of his fits — how else shall I term them? — of enthusiasm. He had found an unknown bivalve, forming a new genus, and, more than this, he had hunted down and secured, with Jupiter's assistance, a *scarabæus* which he believed to be totally new, but in respect to which he wished to have my opinion on the morrow.

"And why not to-night?" I asked, rubbing my hands

1 *

over the blaze, and wishing the whole tribe of *scarabæi* at the devil.

"Ah, if I had only known you were here!" said Legrand, "but it 's so long since I saw you; and how could I foresee that you would pay me a visit this very night of all others? As I was coming home I met Lieutenant G——, from the fort, and, very foolishly, I lent him the bug; so it will be impossible for you to see it until the morning. Stay here to-night, and I will send Jup down for it at sunrise. It is the loveliest thing in creation!"

"What? — sunrise?"

"Nonsense! no! — the bug. It is of a brilliant gold color, — about the size of a large hickory-nut, — with two jet-black spots near one extremity of the back, and another, somewhat longer, at the other. The *antennæ* are —"

"Dey aint *no* tin in him, Massa Will, I keep a tellin on you," here interrupted Jupiter; "de bug is a goole-bug, solid, ebery bit of him, inside and all, sep him wing, — neber feel half so hebby a bug in my life."

"Well, suppose it is, Jup," replied Legrand, somewhat more earnestly, it seemed to me, than the case demanded, "is that any reason for your letting the birds burn? The color" — here he turned to me — "is really almost enough to warrant Jupiter's idea. You never saw a more brilliant metallic lustre than the scales emit, — but of this you cannot judge till to-morrow. In the mean time I can give you some idea of the shape." Saying this, he seated himself at a small table, on which

were a pen and ink, but no paper. He looked for some
in a drawer, but found none.

"Never mind," said he at length, "this will answer";
and he drew from his waistcoat-pocket a scrap of what
I took to be very dirty foolscap, and made upon it a
rough drawing with the pen. While he did this, I retained my seat by the fire, for I was still chilly. When
the design was complete, he handed it to me without
rising. As I received it, a loud growl was heard, succeeded by a scratching at the door. Jupiter opened it,
and a large Newfoundland, belonging to Legrand, rushed
in, leaped upon my shoulders, and loaded me with ca-
resses; for I had shown him much attention during previous visits. When his gambols were over, I looked at
the paper, and, to speak the truth, found myself not a
little puzzled at what my friend had depicted.

"Well!" I said, after contemplating it for some minutes, "this *is* a strange *scarabæus*, I must confess: new
to me: never saw anything like it before, — unless it
was a skull, or a death's-head, — which it more nearly
resembles than anything else that has come under *my*
observation."

"A death's-head!" echoed Legrand — "O — yes —
well, it has something of that appearance upon paper,
no doubt. The two upper black spots look like eyes,
eh? and the longer one at the bottom like a mouth, —
and then the shape of the whole is oval."

"Perhaps so," said I; "but, Legrand, I fear you
are no artist. I must wait until I see the beetle itself, if
I am to form any idea of its personal appearance."

"Well, I don't know," said he, a little nettled, "I

draw tolerably, — *should* do it at least, — have had good masters, and flatter myself that I am not quite a block-head."

"But, my dear fellow, you are joking, then," said I, "this is a very passable *skull*, — indeed, I may say that it is a very *excellent* skull, according to the vulgar notions about such specimens of physiology, — and your *scarabæus* must be the queerest *scarabæus* in the world if it resembles it. Why, we may get up a very thrilling bit of superstition upon this hint. I presume you will call the bug *scarabæus caput hominis,* or something of that kind, — there are many similar titles in the Natural Histories. But where are the *antennæ* you spoke of?"

"The *antennæ!*" said Legrand, who seemed to be getting unaccountably warm upon the subject; "I am sure you must see the *antennæ.* I made them as distinct as they are in the original insect, and I presume that is sufficient."

"Well, well," I said, "perhaps you have, — still I don't see them"; and I handed him the paper without additional remark, not wishing to ruffle his temper; but I was much surprised at the turn affairs had taken; his ill-humor puzzled me; and, as for the drawing of the beetle, there were positively *no antennæ* visible, and the whole *did* bear a very close resemblance to the ordinary cuts of a death's-head.

He received the paper very peevishly, and was about to crumple it, apparently to throw it in the fire, when a casual glance at the design seemed suddenly to rivet his attention. In an instant his face grew violently red, — in another as excessively pale. For some minutes he continued to scrutinize the drawing minutely where he sat. At length he arose, took a candle from the table, and proceeded to seat himself upon a sea-chest in the farthest corner of the room. Here again he made an anxious examination of the paper, turning it in all directions. He said nothing, however, and his conduct greatly astonished me; yet I thought it prudent not to exacerbate the growing moodiness of his temper by any comment. Presently he took from his coat-pocket a wallet, placed the paper carefully in it, and deposited both in a writing-desk, which he locked. He now grew more composed in his demeanor; but his original air of enthusiasm had quite disappeared. Yet he seemed not so much sulky as abstracted. As the evening wore away he became more and more absorbed in revery, from which no sallies of mine could arouse him. It had been my intention to pass the night at the hut, as I had frequently done before, but, seeing my host in this mood, I deemed it proper to take leave. He did not press me to remain, but, as I departed, he shook my hand with even more than his usual cordiality.

It was about a month after this (and during the interval I had seen nothing of Legrand) when I received a visit, at Charleston, from his man, Jupiter. I had never seen the good old negro look so dispirited, and I feared that some serious disaster had befallen my friend.

"Well, Jup," said I, "what is the matter now? — how is your master?"

"Why, to speak de troof, massa, him not so berry well as mought be."

"Not well! I am truly sorry to hear it. What does he complain of?"

"Dar! dat's it!—him neber plain of notin,—but him berry sick for all dat."

"*Very* sick, Jupiter!—why did n't you say so at once? Is he confined to bed?"

"No, dat he aint!—he aint find nowhar,—dat's just whar de shoe pinch,—my mind is got to be berry hebby bout poor Massa Will."

"Jupiter, I should like to understand what it is you are talking about. You say your master is sick. Has n't he told you what ails him?"

"Why, massa, taint worf while for to git mad about de matter,—Massa Will say noffin at all aint de matter wid him,—but den what make him go about looking dis here way, wid he head down and he soldiers up, and as white as a gose? And den he keep a syphon all de time—"

"Keeps a what, Jupiter?"

"Keeps a syphon wid de figgurs on de slate,—de queerest figgurs I ebber did see. Ise gittin to be skeered, I tell you. Hab for to keep mighty tight eye pon him noovers. Todder day he gib me slip fore de sun up and was gone de whole ob de blessed day. I had a big stick ready cut for to gib him deuced good beating when he did come,—but Ise sich a fool dat I had n't de heart arter all,—he look so berry poorly."

"Eh?—what?—ah yes!—upon the whole I think you had better not be too severe with the poor fellow,—don't flog him, Jupiter,—he can't very well stand it,—but can you form no idea of what has occasioned this illness, or rather this change of conduct? Has anything unpleasant happened since I saw you?"

"No, massa, dey aint bin noffin onpleasant *since* den, — 't was *fore* den I 'm feared, — 't was de berry day you was dare."

"How? what do you mean?"

"Why, massa, I mean de bug — dare now."

"The what?"

"De bug, — I 'm berry sartain dat Massa Will bin bit somewhere bout de head by dat goole-bug."

"And what cause have you, Jupiter, for such a supposition?"

"Claws enuff, massa, and mouff too. I nebber did see sich a deuced bug, — he kick and he bite ebery ting what cum near him. Massa Will cotch him fuss, but had for to let him go gin mighty quick, I tell you — den was de time he must ha got de bite. I did n't like de look ob de bug mouff, myself, no how, so I would n't take hold ob him wid my finger, but I cotch him wid a piece ob paper dat I found. I rap him up in de paper and stuff piece ob it in he mouff, — dat was de way."

"And you think, then, that your master was really bitten by the beetle, and that the bite made him sick?"

"I don't tink noffin about it, — I nose it. What make him dream bout de goole so much, if taint cause he bit by de goole-bug? Ise heerd bout dem goole-bugs fore dis."

"But how do you know he dreams about gold?"

"How I know? why cause he talk about it in he sleep, — dat 's how I nose."

"Well, Jup, perhaps you are right; but to what for-

tunate circumstance am I to attribute the honor of a visit
from you to-day ? "

"What de matter, massa ? "

"Did you bring any message from Mr. Legrand ? "

"No, massa, I bring dis here pissel"; and here Jupiter
handed me a note which ran thus : —

MY DEAR ——: Why have I not seen you for so long a
time ? I hope you have not been so foolish as to take offence
at any little *brusquerie* of mine ; but no, that is improbable.

Since I saw you I have had great cause for anxiety. I have
something to tell you, yet scarcely know how to tell it, or
whether I should tell it at all.

I have not been quite well for some days past, and poor old
Jup annoys me, almost beyond endurance, by his well-meant
attentions. Would you believe it ? — he had prepared a huge
stick, the other day, with which to chastise me for giving him
the slip, and spending the day, *solus*, among the hills on the
mainland. I verily believe that my ill looks alone saved me a
flogging.

I have made no addition to my cabinet since we met.

If you can in any way make it convenient, come over with
Jupiter. *Do* come. I wish to see you *to-night*, upon business
of importance. I assure you that it is of the *highest* importance.   Ever yours,

WILLIAM LEGRAND.

There was something in the tone of this note which
gave me great uneasiness. Its whole style differed
materially from that of Legrand. What could he be
dreaming of ? What new crotchet possessed his excita-
ble brain ? What "business of the highest importance"
could *he* possibly have to transact ? Jupiter's account

of him boded no good. I dreaded lest the continued pressure of misfortune had, at length, fairly unsettled the reason of my friend. Without a moment's hesitation, therefore, I prepared to accompany the negro.

Upon reaching the wharf, I noticed a scythe and three spades, all apparently new, lying in the bottom of the boat in which we were to embark.

"What is the meaning of all this, Jup?" I inquired.

"Him syfe, massa, and spade."

"Very true; but what are they doing here?"

"Him de syfe and de spade what Massa Will sis pon my buying for him in de town, and de debbil's own lot of money I had to gib for em."

"But what, in the name of all that is mysterious, is your 'Massa Will' going to do with scythes and spades?"

"Dat's more dan *I* know, and debbil take me if I don't blieve 't is more dan he know, too. But it's all cum ob de bug."

Finding that no satisfaction was to be obtained of Jupiter, whose whole intellect seemed to be absorbed by "de bug," I now stepped into the boat and made sail. With a fair and strong breeze we soon ran into the little cove to the northward of Fort Moultrie, and a walk of some two miles brought us to the hut. It was about three in the afternoon when we arrived. Legrand had been awaiting us in eager expectation. He grasped my hand with a nervous *empressement* which alarmed me and strengthened the suspicions already entertained. His countenance was pale even to ghastliness, and his deep-set eyes glared with unnatural lustre. After some in-

B

quiries respecting his health, I asked him, not knowing what better to say, if he had yet obtained the *scarabæus* from Lieutenant G——.

"O yes," he replied, coloring violently, "I got it from him the next morning. Nothing should tempt me to part with that *scarabæus*. Do you know that Jupiter is quite right about it?"

"In what way?" I asked, with a sad foreboding at heart.

"In supposing it to be a bug of *real gold*." He said this with an air of profound seriousness, and I felt inexpressibly shocked.

"This bug is to make my fortune," he continued, with a triumphant smile, "to reinstate me in my family possessions. Is it any wonder, then, that I prize it? Since Fortune has thought fit to bestow it upon me, I have only to use it properly and I shall arrive at the gold of which it is the index. Jupiter, bring me that *scarabæus!*"

"What! de bug, massa? I'd rudder not go fer trubble dat bug, — you mus git him for your own self." Hereupon Legrand arose, with a grave and stately air, and brought me the beetle from a glass case in which it was enclosed. It was a beautiful *scarabæus*, and, at that time, unknown to naturalists, — of course a great prize in a scientific point of view. There were two round black spots near one extremity of the back, and a long one near the other. The scales were exceedingly hard and glossy, with all the appearance of burnished gold. The weight of the insect was very remarkable, and, taking all things into consideration, I could hardly blame Jupiter for his opinion respecting it; but what to make of Legrand's concordance with that opinion I could not for the life of me tell.

"I sent for you," said he, in a grandiloquent tone, when I had completed my examination of the beetle, — "I sent for you, that I might have your counsel and assistance in furthering the views of Fate and of the bug — "

"My dear Legrand," I cried, interrupting him, "you are certainly unwell, and had better use some little precautions. You shall go to bed, and I will remain with you a few days, until you get over this. You are feverish and — "

"Feel my pulse," said he.

I felt it, and, to say the truth, found not the slightest indication of fever.

"But you may be ill and yet have no fever. Allow me this once to prescribe for you. In the first place, go to bed. In the next — "

"You are mistaken," he interposed; "I am as well as I can expect to be under the excitement which I suffer. If you really wish me well, you will relieve this excitement."

"And how is this to be done?"

"Very easily. Jupiter and myself are going upon an expedition into the hills, upon the mainland, and, in this expedition, we shall need the aid of some person in whom we can confide. You are the only one we can trust. Whether we succeed or fail, the excitement which you now perceive in me will be equally allayed."

"I am anxious to oblige you in any way," I replied;

"but do you mean to say that this infernal beetle has any connection with your expedition into the hills?"

"It has."

"Then, Legrand, I can become a party to no such absurd proceeding."

"I am sorry — very sorry — for we shall have to try it by ourselves."

"Try it by yourselves! The man is surely mad! — but stay! — how long do you propose to be absent?"

"Probably all night. We shall start immediately, and be back, at all events, by sunrise."

"And will you promise me, upon your honor, that when this freak of yours is over, and the bug business (good God!) settled to your satisfaction, you will then return home and follow my advice implicitly, as that of your physician?"

"Yes; I promise; and now let us be off, for we have no time to lose."

With a heavy heart I accompanied my friend. We started about four o'clock, — Legrand, Jupiter, the dog, and myself. Jupiter had with him the scythe and spades, the whole of which he insisted upon carrying, — more through fear, it seemed to me, of trusting either of the implements within reach of his master, than from any excess of industry or complaisance. His demeanor was dogged in the extreme, and "dat deuced bug" were the sole words which escaped his lips during the journey. For my own part, I had charge of a couple of dark-lanterns, while Legrand contented himself with the *scarabæus*, which he carried attached to the end of a bit of whip-cord; twirling it to and fro, with the air of a conjurer, as he went. When I observed this last plain evidence of my friend's aberration of mind, I could scarcely refrain from tears. I thought it best, however, to humor his fancy, at least for the present, or until I could adopt some more energetic measures with a chance of success. In the mean time I endeavored, but all in vain, to sound him in regard to the object of the expedition. Having succeeded in inducing me to accompany him, he seemed unwilling to hold conversation upon any topic of minor importance, and to all my questions vouchsafed no other reply than " we shall see ! "

We crossed the creek at the head of the island by means of a skiff, and, ascending the high grounds on the shore of the mainland, proceeded in a northwesterly direction, through a tract of country excessively wild and desolate, where no trace of a human footstep was to be seen. Legrand led the way with decision; pausing only for an instant, here and there, to consult what appeared to be certain landmarks of his own contrivance upon a former occasion.

In this manner we journeyed for about two hours, and the sun was just setting when we entered a region infinitely more dreary than any yet seen. It was a species of table-land, near the summit of an almost inaccessible hill, densely wooded from base to pinnacle, and interspersed with huge crags that appeared to lie loosely upon the soil, and in many cases were prevented from precipitating themselves into the valleys below, merely by the support of the trees against which they reclined. Deep ravines, in various directions, gave an air of still sterner solemnity to the scene.

The natural platform to which we had clambered was
thickly overgrown with brambles, through which we soon
discovered that it would have been impossible to force
our way but for the scythe; and Jupiter, by direction of
his master, proceeded to clear for us a path to the foot
of an enormously tall tulip-tree, which stood, with some
eight or ten oaks, upon the level, and far surpassed them
all, and all other trees which I had then ever seen, in the
beauty of its foliage and form, in the wide spread of its
branches, and in the general majesty of its appearance.
When we reached this tree, Legrand turned to Jupiter,
and asked him if he thought he could climb it. The old
man seemed a little staggered by the question, and for
some moments made no reply. At length he approached
the huge trunk, walked slowly around it, and examined
it with minute attention. When he had completed his
scrutiny, he merely said, —

"Yes, massa, Jup climb any tree he ebber see in he
life."

"Then up with you as soon as possible, for it will
soon be too dark to see what we are about."

"How far mus go up, massa?" inquired Jupiter.

"Get up the main trunk first, and then I will you
tell you which way to go — and here — stop! take this
beetle with you."

"De bug, Massa Will! — de goole-bug!" cried the
negro, drawing back in dismay — "what for mus tote de
bug way up de tree? — d—n if I do!"

"If you are afraid, Jup, a great big negro like you,
to take hold of a harmless little dead beetle, why you
can carry it up by this string; but, if you do not take

it up with you in some way, I shall be under the necessity of breaking your head with this shovel."

"What de matter now, massa?" said Jup, evidently shamed into compliance; "always want for to raise fuss wid old nigger. Was only funnin anyhow. *Me* feered de bug! what I keer for de bug?" Here he took cautiously hold of the extreme end of the string, and, maintaining the insect as far from his person as circumstances would permit, prepared to ascend the tree.

In youth, the tulip-tree, or *Liriodendron tulipiferum,* the most magnificent of American foresters, has a trunk peculiarly smooth, and often rises to a great height without lateral branches; but, in its riper age, the bark becomes gnarled and uneven, while many short limbs make their appearance on the stem. Thus the difficulty of ascension, in the present case, lay more in semblance than in reality. Embracing the huge cylinder, as closely as possible, with his arms and knees, seizing with his hands some projections, and resting his naked toes upon others, Jupiter, after one or two narrow escapes from falling, at length wriggled himself into the first great fork, and seemed to consider the whole business as virtually accomplished. The *risk* of the achievement was, in fact, now over, although the climber was some sixty or seventy feet from the ground.

"Which way mus go now, Massa Will?" he asked.

"Keep up the largest branch, — the one on this side," said Legrand. The negro obeyed him promptly, and apparently with but little trouble; ascending higher and higher, until no glimpse of his squat figure could be

obtained through the dense foliage which enveloped it.
Presently his voice was heard in a sort of halloo.

"How much fudder is got for go?"

"How high up are you?" asked Legrand.

"Ebber so fur," replied the negro; "can see de sky
fru de top ob de tree."

"Never mind the sky, but attend to what I say.
Look down the trunk and count the limbs below you on
this side. How many limbs have you passed?"

"One, two, tree, four, fibe, — I done pass fibe big
limb, massa, pon dis side."

"Then go one limb higher."

In a few minutes the voice was heard again, announcing that the seventh limb was attained.

"Now, Jup," cried Legrand, evidently much excited,
"I want you to work your way out upon that limb as far
as you can. If you see anything strange, let me know."

By this time what little doubt I might have entertained
of my poor friend's insanity was put finally at rest. I
had no alternative but to conclude him stricken with
lunacy, and I became seriously anxious about getting
him home. While I was pondering upon what was best
to be done, Jupiter's voice was again heard.

"Mos feerd for to ventur pon dis limb berry far, —
't is dead limb putty much all de way."

"Did you say it was a *dead* limb, Jupiter?" cried
Legrand in a quavering voice.

"Yes, massa, him dead as de door-nail — done up for
sartain — done departed dis here life."

"What in the name of Heaven shall I do?" asked
Legrand, seemingly in the greatest distress.

"Do!" said I, glad of an opportunity to interpose a word; "why come home and go to bed. Come, now! — that's a fine fellow. It's getting late, and, besides, you remember your promise."

"Jupiter," cried he, without heeding me in the least, "do you hear me?"

"Yes, Massa Will, hear you ebber so plain."

"Try the wood well, then, with your knife, and see if you think it *very* rotten."

"Him rotten, massa, sure nuff," replied the negro in a few moments, "but not so berry rotten as mought be. Mought ventur out leetle way pon de limb by myself, dat's true."

"By yourself! — what do you mean?"

"Why I mean de bug. 'T is *berry* hebby bug. Spose I drop him down fuss, and den de limb won't break wid just de weight ob one nigger."

"You infernal scoundrel!" cried Legrand, apparently much relieved, "what do you mean by telling me such nonsense as that? As sure as you drop that beetle I'll break your neck. Look here, Jupiter, do you hear me?"

"Yes, massa, need n't hollo at poor nigger dat style."

"Well! now listen! — if you will venture out on the limb as far as you think safe, and not let go the beetle, I'll make you a present of a silver dollar as soon as you get down."

"I'm gwine, Massa Will, — deed I is," replied the negro very promptly, — "mos out to the eend now."

"*Out to the end!*" here fairly screamed Legrand; "do you say you are out to the end of that limb?"

"Soon be to de eend, massa, — o-o-o-o-oh! Lor-gol-a-marcy! what *is* dis here pon de tree?"

"Well!" cried Legrand, highly delighted, "what is it?"

"Why, taint noffin but a skull — somebody bin lef him head up de tree, and de crows done gobble ebery bit ob de meat off."

"A skull, you say! — very well! — how is it fastened to the limb? — what holds it on?"

"Sure nuff, massa; mus look. Why dis berry curous sarcumstance, pon my word, — dare's a great big nail in de skull, what fastens ob it on to de tree."

"Well, now, Jupiter, do exactly as I tell you, — do you hear?"

"Yes, massa."

"Pay attention, then! — find the left eye of the skull."

"Hum! hoo! dat's good! why, dare aint no eye lef at all."

"Curse your stupidity! do you know your right hand from your left?"

"Yes, I nose dat, — nose all bout dat, — 't is my lef hand what I chops de wood wid."

"To be sure! you are left-handed; and your left eye is on the same side as your left hand. Now, I suppose, you can find the left eye of the skull, or the place where the left eye has been. Have you found it?"

Here was a long pause. At length the negro asked, —

"Is de lef eye of de skull pon de same side as de lef hand of de skull, too? — cause de skull aint got not a

bit ob a hand at all, — nebber mind ! I got de lef eye
now, — here de lef eye ! what mus do wid it ? "

"Let the beetle drop through it, as far as the string
will reach, — but be careful and not let go your hold of
the string."

"All dat done, Massa Will; mighty easy ting for to
put de bug fru de hole, — look out for him dare below ! "

During this colloquy no portion of Jupiter's person
could be seen; but the beetle, which he had suffered to
descend, was now visible at the end of the string, and
glistened, like a globe of burnished gold, in the last rays
of the setting sun, some of which still faintly illumined
the eminence upon which we stood. The *scarabæus*
hung quite clear of any branches, and, if allowed to fall,
would have fallen at our feet. Legrand immediately
took the scythe, and cleared with it a circular space,
three or four yards in diameter, just beneath the insect,
and, having accomplished this, ordered Jupiter to let go
the string and come down from the tree.

Driving a peg, with great nicety, into the ground, at
the precise spot where the beetle fell, my friend now produced from his pocket a tape-measure. Fastening one
end of this at that point of the trunk of the tree which
was nearest the peg, he unrolled it till it reached the peg,
and thence farther unrolled it, in the direction already
established by the two points of the tree and the peg,
for the distance of fifty feet, — Jupiter clearing away the
brambles with the scythe. At the spot thus attained
a second peg was driven, and about this, as a centre,
a rude circle, about four feet in diameter, described.
Taking now a spade himself, and giving one to Jupiter

and one to me, Legrand begged us to set about digging as quickly as possible.

To speak the truth, I had no especial relish for such amusement at any time, and, at that particular moment, would most willingly have declined it; for the night was coming on, and I felt much fatigued with the exercise already taken; but I saw no mode of escape, and was fearful of disturbing my poor friend's equanimity by a refusal. Could I have depended, indeed, upon Jupiter's aid, I would have had no hesitation in attempting to get the lunatic home by force; but I was too well assured of the old negro's disposition, to hope that he would assist me, under any circumstances, in a personal contest with his master. I made no doubt that the latter had been infected with some of the innumerable Southern superstitions about money buried, and that his fantasy had received confirmation by the finding of the *scarabæus*, or, perhaps, by Jupiter's obstinacy in maintaining it to be "a bug of real gold." A mind disposed to lunacy would readily be led away by such suggestions, — especially if chiming in with favorite preconceived ideas, — and then I called to mind the poor fellow's speech about the beetle's being "the index of his fortune." Upon the whole, I was sadly vexed and puzzled, but, at length, I concluded to make a virtue of necessity, — to dig with a good will, and thus the sooner to convince the visionary, by ocular demonstration, of the fallacy of the opinions he entertained.

The lanterns having been lit, we all fell to work with a zeal worthy a more rational cause; and, as the glare fell upon our persons and implements, I could not help thinking how picturesque a group we composed, and how strange and suspicious our labors must have appeared to any interloper who, by chance, might have stumbled upon our whereabouts.

We dug very steadily for two hours. Little was said; and our chief embarrassment lay in the yelpings of the dog, who took exceeding interest in our proceedings. He, at length, became so obstreperous that we grew fearful of his giving the alarm to some stragglers in the vicinity ; — or, rather, this was the apprehension of Legrand ; — for myself, I should have rejoiced at any interruption which might have enabled me to get the wanderer home. The noise was, at length, very effectually silenced by Jupiter, who, getting out of the hole with a dogged air of deliberation, tied the brute's mouth up with one of his suspenders, and then returned, with a grave chuckle, to his task.

When the time mentioned had expired, we had reached a depth of five feet, and yet no signs of any treasure became manifest. A general pause ensued, and I began to hope that the farce was at an end. Legrand, however, although evidently much disconcerted, wiped his brow thoughtfully and recommenced. We had excavated the entire circle of four feet diameter, and now we slightly enlarged the limit, and went to the farther depth of two feet. Still nothing appeared. The gold-seeker, whom I sincerely pitied, at length clambered from the pit, with the bitterest disappointment imprinted upon every feature, and proceeded, slowly and reluctantly, to put on his coat, which he had thrown off at the beginning of his labor. In the mean time I made no remark. Jupiter, at a signal from his master, began to gather up his tools. This done, and the dog having been unmuzzled, we turned in profound silence towards home.

We had taken, perhaps, a dozen steps in this direction, when, with a loud oath, Legrand strode up to Jupiter, and seized him by the collar. The astonished negro opened his eyes and mouth to the fullest extent, let fall the spades, and fell upon his knees.

"You scoundrel," said Legrand, hissing out the syllables from between his clinched teeth, — "you infernal black villain! — speak, I tell you! — answer me this instant, without prevarication! — which — which is your left eye?"

"O, my golly, Massa Will! aint dis here my lef eye for sartin?" roared the terrified Jupiter, placing his hand upon his *right* organ of vision, and holding it there with a desperate pertinacity, as if in immediate dread of his master's attempt at a gouge.

"I thought so! — I knew it! hurrah!" vociferated Legrand, letting the negro go, and executing a series of curvets and caracoles, much to the astonishment of his valet, who, arising from his knees, looked, mutely, from his master to myself, and then from myself to his master.

"Come! we must go back," said the latter, "the game's not up yet." And he again led the way to the tulip-tree.

"Jupiter," said he, when we reached its foot, "come here! Was the skull nailed to the limb with the face outwards, or with the face to the limb?"

" De face was out, massa, so dat de crows could get at de eyes good, widout any trouble."

" Well, then, was it this eye or that through which you dropped the beetle ? " — here Legrand touched each of Jupiter's eyes.

" 'T was dis eye, massa, — de lef eye, — jis as you tell me," and here it was his right eye that the negro indicated.

" That will do, — we must try it again."

Here my friend, about whose madness I now saw, or fancied that I saw, certain indications of method, re- moved the peg which marked the spot where the beetle fell, to a spot about three inches to the westward of its former position. Taking, now, the tape-measure from the nearest point of the trunk to the peg, as before, and continuing the extension in a straight line to the distance of fifty feet, a spot was indicated, removed, by several yards, from the point at which we had been digging.

Around the new position a circle, somewhat larger than in the former instance, was now described, and we again set to work with the spades. I was dreadfully weary, but, scarcely understanding what had occasioned the change in my thoughts, I felt no longer any great aversion from the labor imposed. I had become most unaccountably interested, — nay, even excited. Perhaps there was something, amid all the extravagant demeanor of Legrand, — some air of forethought, or of delibera- tion, — which impressed me. I dug eagerly, and now and then caught myself actually looking, with something that very much resembled expectation, for the fancied treasure, the vision of which had demented my unfortu-

nate companion. At a period when such vagaries of
thought most fully possessed me, and when we had been
at work perhaps an hour and a half, we were again interrupted by the violent howlings of the dog. His uneasiness, in the first instance, had been, evidently, but the
result of playfulness or caprice, but he now assumed a
bitter and serious tone. Upon Jupiter's again attempting to muzzle him, he made furious resistance, and,
leaping into the hole, tore up the mould frantically with
his claws. In a few seconds he had uncovered a mass
of human bones, forming two complete skeletons, inter-
mingled with several buttons of metal, and what appeared to be the dust of decayed woollen. One or two
strokes of a spade upturned the blade of a large Spanish
knife, and, as we dug farther, three or four loose pieces
of gold and silver coin came to light.

At sight of these, the joy of Jupiter could scarcely be
restrained, but the countenance of his master wore an
air of extreme disappointment. He urged us, however,
to continue our exertions, and the words were hardly
uttered, when I stumbled and fell forward, having caught
the toe of my boot in a large ring of iron that lay half
buried in the loose earth.

We now worked in earnest, and never did I pass ten
minutes of more intense excitement. During this interval we had fairly unearthed an oblong chest of wood,
which, from its perfect preservation and wonderful
hardness, had plainly been subjected to some mineraliz-
ing process, — perhaps that of the bichloride of mer-
cury. This box was three feet and a half long, three
feet broad, and two and a half feet deep. It was firmly

secured by bands of wrought-iron, riveted, and forming
a kind of open trellis-work over the whole. On each
side of the chest, near the top, were three rings of iron,
— six in all, — by means of which a firm hold could be
obtained by six persons. Our utmost united endeavors
served only to disturb the coffer very slightly in its bed.
We at once saw the impossibility of removing so great
a weight. Luckily, the sole fastenings of the lid consisted of two sliding bolts. These we drew back, —
trembling and panting with anxiety. In an instant, a
treasure of incalculable value lay gleaming before us.
As the rays of the lanterns fell within the pit, there
flashed upwards a glow and a glare, from a confused
heap of gold and of jewels, that absolutely dazzled our
eyes.

I shall not pretend to describe the feelings with which
I gazed. Amazement was, of course, predominant. Legrand appeared exhausted with excitement, and spoke
very few words. Jupiter's countenance wore, for some
minutes, as deadly a pallor as it is possible, in the nature of things, for any negro's visage to assume. He
seemed stupefied, — thunder-stricken. Presently he fell
upon his knees in the pit, and, burying his naked arms
up to the elbows in gold, let them there remain, as if
enjoying the luxury of a bath. At length, with a deep
sigh, he exclaimed, as if in a soliloquy, —

"And dis all cum ob de goole-bug! de putty goole-
bug! de poor little goole-bug, what I boosed in dat
sabage kind ob style! Aint you shamed ob yourself, nigger? — answer me dat!"

It became necessary, at last, that I should arouse both

2 *

master and valet to the expediency of removing the treasure. It was growing late, and it behooved us to make exertion, that we might get everything housed before daylight. It was difficult to say what should be done, and much time was spent in deliberation, — so confused were the ideas of all. We finally lightened the box by removing two thirds of its contents, when we were enabled, with some trouble, to raise it from the hole. The articles taken out were deposited among the brambles, and the dog left to guard them, with strict orders from Jupiter neither, upon any pretence, to stir from the spot, nor to open his mouth until our return. We then hurriedly made for home with the chest; reaching the hut in safety, but after excessive toil, at one o'clock in the morning. Worn out as we were, it was not in human nature to do more immediately. We rested until two, and had supper; starting for the hills immediately afterwards, armed with three stout sacks, which, by good luck, were upon the premises. A little before four we arrived at the pit, divided the remainder of the booty, as equally as might be, among us, and, leaving the holes unfilled, again set out for the hut, at which, for the second time, we deposited our golden burdens, just as the first faint streaks of the dawn gleamed from over the tree-tops in the east.

We were now thoroughly broken down; but the intense excitement of the time denied us repose. After an unquiet slumber of some three or four hours' duration, we arose, as if by preconcert, to make examination of our treasure.

The chest had been full to the brim, and we spent the

whole day and the greater part of the next night in a
scrutiny of its contents. There had been nothing like
order or arrangement. Everything had been heaped in
promiscuously. Having assorted all with care, we found
ourselves possessed of even vaster wealth than we had
at first supposed. In coin there was rather more than
four hundred and fifty thousand dollars, — estimating
the value of the pieces, as accurately as we could, by
the tables of the period. There was not a particle of
silver. All was gold of antique date and of great va-
riety, — French, Spanish, and German money, with a
few English guineas, and some counters, of which we
had never seen specimens before. There were several
very large and heavy coins, so worn that we could make
nothing of their inscriptions. There was no American
money. The value of the jewels we found more difficulty in estimating. There were diamonds, — some of
them exceedingly large and fine, — a hundred and ten
in all, and not one of them small; eighteen rubies of remarkable brilliancy; three hundred and ten emeralds,
all very beautiful; and twenty-one sapphires, with an
opal. These stones had all been broken from their settings and thrown loose in the chest. The settings themselves, which we picked out from among the other gold,
appeared to have been beaten up with hammers, as if to
prevent identification. Besides all this, there was a vast
quantity of solid gold ornaments; — nearly two hundred
massive finger and ear rings; — rich chains, — thirty of
these, if I remember; — eighty-three very large and
heavy crucifixes; — five gold censers of great value; —
a prodigious golden punch-bowl, ornamented with richly

chased vine-leaves and Bacchanalian figures; with two sword-handles exquisitely embossed, and many other smaller articles which I cannot recollect. The weight of these valuables exceeded three hundred and fifty pounds avoirdupois; and in this estimate I have not included one hundred and ninety-seven superb gold watches; three of the number being worth each five hundred dollars, if one. Many of them were very old, and as time-keepers valueless; the works having suffered, more or less, from corrosion, — but all were richly jewelled and in cases of great worth. We estimated the entire contents of the chest, that night, at a million and a half of dollars; and, upon the subsequent disposal of the trinkets and jewels (a few being retained for our own use), it was found that we had greatly undervalued the treasure.

When, at length, we had concluded our examination, and the intense excitement of the time had in some measure subsided, Legrand, who saw that I was dying with impatience for a solution of this most extraordinary riddle, entered into a full detail of all the circumstances connected with it.

" You remember," said he, " the night when I handed you the rough sketch I had made of the *scarabæus*. You recollect, also, that I became quite vexed at you for insisting that my drawing resembled a death's-head. When you first made this assertion I thought you were jesting; but afterwards I called to mind the peculiar spots on the back of the insect, and admitted to myself that your remark had some little foundation in fact. Still, the sneer at my graphic powers irritated me, — for I am considered a good artist, — and, therefore, when you handed me the scrap of parchment, I was about to crumple it up and throw it angrily into the fire."

" The scrap of paper, you mean," said I.

" No ; it had much of the appearance of paper, and at first I supposed it to be such, but when I came to draw upon it, I discovered it, at once, to be a piece of very thin parchment. It was quite dirty, you remember. Well, as I was in the very act of crumpling it up, my glance fell upon the sketch at which you had been looking, and you may imagine my astonishment when I perceived, in fact, the figure of a death's-head just where, it seemed to me, I had made the drawing of the beetle. For a moment I was too much amazed to think with accuracy. I knew that my design was very different in detail from this, — although there was a certain similarity in general outline. Presently I took a candle, and seating myself at the other end of the room, proceeded to scrutinize the parchment more closely. Upon turning it over, I saw my own sketch upon the reverse, just as I had made it. My first idea, now, was mere surprise at the really remarkable similarity of outline, — at the singular coincidence involved in the fact that, unknown to me, there should have been a skull upon the other side of the parchment, immediately beneath my figure of the *scarabæus*, and that his skull, not only in outline, but in size, should so closely resemble my drawing. I say the singularity of this coincidence absolutely stupefied me for a time. This is the usual effect of such coincidences. The mind struggles to establish a connection, — a sequence of cause and effect, — and, being unable

to do so, suffers a species of temporary paralysis. But,
when I recovered from this stupor, there dawned upon
me gradually a conviction which startled me even far
more than the coincidence. I began distinctly, positively,
to remember that there had been *no* drawing upon the
parchment when I made my sketch of the *scarabæus*.
I became perfectly certain of this; for I recollected
turning up first one side and then the other, in search
of the cleanest spot. Had the skull been there then, of
course I could not have failed to notice it. Here was
indeed a mystery which I felt it impossible to explain;
but, even at that early moment, there seemed to glimmer,
faintly, within the most remote and secret chambers of
my intellect, a glow-worm-like conception of that truth
which last night's adventure brought to so magnificent
a demonstration. I arose at once, and putting the
parchment securely away, dismissed all further reflection
until I should be alone.

"When you had gone, and when Jupiter was fast
asleep, I betook myself to a more methodical investiga-
tion of the affair. In the first place I considered the
manner in which the parchment had come into my possession. The spot where we discovered the *scarabæus*
was on the coast of the mainland, about a mile eastward of the island, and but a short distance above high-
water mark. Upon my taking hold of it, it gave me
a sharp bite, which caused me to let it drop. Jupiter,
with his accustomed caution, before seizing the insect,
which had flown towards him, looked about him for a
leaf, or something of that nature, by which to take hold
of it. It was at this moment that his eyes, and mine

also, fell upon the scrap of parchment, which I then supposed to be paper. It was lying half buried in the sand,
a corner sticking up. Near the spot where we found it
I observed the remnants of the hull of what appeared to
have been a ship's long-boat. The wreck seemed to
have been there for a very great while; for the resemblance to boat timbers could scarcely be traced.

"Well, Jupiter picked up the parchment, wrapped
the beetle in it, and gave it to me. Soon afterwards we
turned to go home, and on the way met Lieutenant
G——. I showed him the insect, and he begged me to let
him take it to the fort. Upon my consenting, he thrust
it forthwith into his waistcoat-pocket, without the parchment in which it had been wrapped, and which I had
continued to hold in my hand during his inspection.
Perhaps he dreaded my changing my mind, and thought
it best to make sure of the prize at once, — you know
how enthusiastic he is on all subjects connected with
Natural History. At the same time, without being conscious of it, I must have deposited the parchment in my
own pocket.

"You remember that when I went to the table, for
the purpose of making a sketch of the beetle, I found
no paper where it was usually kept. I looked in the
drawer, and found none there. I searched my pockets,
hoping to find an old letter, when my hand fell upon the
parchment. I thus detail the precise mode in which it
came into my possession; for the circumstances impressed
me with peculiar force.

"No doubt you will think me fanciful, — but I had
already established a kind of *connection*. I had put

together two links of a great chain. There was a boat
lying upon a sea-coast, and not far from the boat was a
parchment — *not a paper* — with a skull depicted upon
it. You will, of course, ask, ' Where is the connection ? '
I reply that the skull, or death's-head, is the well-known
emblem of the pirate. The flag of the death's-head is
hoisted in all engagements.

"I have said that the scrap was parchment, and not
paper. Parchment is durable, — almost imperishable.
Matters of little moment are rarely consigned to parchment; since, for the mere ordinary purposes of drawing
or writing, it is not nearly so well adapted as paper.
This reflection suggested some meaning — some rele-
vancy — in the death's-head. I did not fail to observe,
also, the *form* of the parchment. Although one of its
corners had been, by some accident, destroyed, it could
be seen that the original form was oblong. It was just
such a slip, indeed, as might have been chosen for a
memorandum, — for a record of something to be long
remembered and carefully preserved."

"But," I interposed, "you say that the skull was *not*
upon the parchment when you made the drawing of the
beetle. How then do you trace any connection between
the boat and the skull, — since this latter, according to
your own admission, must have been designed (God only
knows how or by whom) at some period subsequent to
your sketching the *scarabæus ?* "

"Ah, hereupon turns the whole mystery; although
the secret, at this point, I had comparatively little difficulty in solving. My steps were sure, and could afford
but a single result. I reasoned, for example, thus:

When I drew the *scarabæus*, there was no skull apparent upon the parchment. When I had completed the drawing I gave it to you, and observed you narrowly until you returned it. *You*, therefore, did not design the skull, and no one else was present to do it. Then it was not done by human agency. And nevertheless it was done.

"At this stage of my reflections I endeavored to remember, and *did* remember, with entire distinctness, every incident which occurred about the period in question. The weather was chilly, (O rare and happy accident!) and a fire was blazing upon the hearth. I was heated with exercise, and sat near the table. You, however, had drawn a chair close to the chimney. Just as I placed the parchment in your hand, and as you were in the act of inspecting it, Wolf, the Newfoundland, entered, and leaped upon your shoulders. With your left hand you caressed him and kept him off, while your right, holding the parchment, was permitted to fall listlessly between your knees, and in close proximity to the fire. At one moment I thought the blaze had caught it, and was about to caution you, but, before I could speak, you had withdrawn it, and were engaged in its examination. When I considered all these particulars, I doubted not for a moment that *heat* had been the agent in bringing to light, upon the parchment, the skull which I saw designed upon it. You are well aware that chemical preparations exist, and have existed time out of mind, by means of which it is possible to write upon either paper or vellum, so that the characters shall become visible only when subjected to the action of fire. Zaffre, digested in

aqua regia, and diluted with four times its weight of
water, is sometimes employed; a green tint results. The
regulus of cobalt, dissolved in spirit of nitre, gives a red.
These colors disappear at longer or shorter intervals after
the material written upon cools, but again become apparent upon the re-application of heat.

"I now scrutinized the death's-head with care. Its
outer edges — the edges of the drawing nearest the edge
of the vellum — were far more *distinct* than the others.
It was clear that the action of the caloric had been im-
perfect or unequal. I immediately kindled a fire, and
subjected every portion of the parchment to a glowing
heat. At first, the only effect was the strengthening of
the faint lines in the skull; but, upon persevering in the
experiment, there became visible, at the corner of the
slip, diagonally opposite to the spot in which the death's-
head was delineated, the figure of what I at first supposed
to be a goat. A closer scrutiny, however, satisfied me
that it was intended for a kid."

"Ha! ha!" said I, "to be sure I have no right to
laugh at you, — a million and a half of money is too
serious a matter for mirth, — but you are not about to
establish a third link in your chain, — you will not find
any especial connection between your pirates and a goat,
— pirates, you know, have nothing to do with goats;
they appertain to the farming interest."

"But I have just said that the figure was *not* that of a
goat."

"Well, a kid then, — pretty much the same thing."

"Pretty much, but not altogether," said Legrand.
"You may have heard of one *Captain* Kidd. I at once

looked upon the figure of the animal as a kind of punning or hieroglyphical signature. I say signature; because its position upon the vellum suggested this idea. The death's-head at the corner diagonally opposite had, in the same manner, the air of a stamp, or seal. But I was sorely put out by the absence of all else — of the body to my imagined instrument — of the text for my context."

"I presume you expected to find a letter between the stamp and the signature."

"Something of that kind. The fact is, I felt irresistibly impressed with a presentiment of some vast good fortune impending. I can scarcely say why. Perhaps, after all, it was rather a desire than an actual belief; — but do you know that Jupiter's silly words, about the bug being of solid gold, had a remarkable effect upon my fancy? And then the series of accidents and coincidences, — these were so *very* extraordinary. Do you observe how mere an accident it was that these events should have occurred upon the *sole* day of all the year in which it has been, or may be, sufficiently cool for fire, and that without the fire, or without the intervention of the dog at the precise moment in which he appeared, I should never have become aware of the death's-head, and so never the possessor of the treasure?"

"But proceed, — I am all impatience."

"Well; you have heard, of course, the many stories current, — the thousand vague rumors afloat about money buried, somewhere upon the Atlantic coast, by Kidd and his associates. These rumors must have had some foundation in fact. And that the rumors have existed so

long and so continuously could have resulted, it appeared
to me, only from the circumstance of the buried treasure
still *remaining* entombed. Had Kidd concealed his plun-
der for a time, and afterwards reclaimed it, the rumors
would scarcely have reached us in their present unvary-
ing form. You will observe that the stories told are all
about money-seekers, not about money-finders. Had the
pirate recovered his money, there the affair would have
dropped. It seemed to me that some accident — say the
loss of a memorandum indicating its locality — had deprived him of the means of recovering it, and that this
accident had become known to his followers, who otherwise might never have heard that treasure had been
concealed at all, and who, busying themselves in vain,
because unguided, attempts to regain it, had given first
birth, and then universal currency, to the reports which
are now so common. Have you ever heard of any important treasure being unearthed along the coast ? "

"Never."

"But that Kidd's accumulations were immense, is well
known. I took it for granted, therefore, that the earth
still held them; and you will scarcely be surprised when
I tell you that I felt a hope, nearly amounting to certainty, that the parchment so strangely found, involved
a lost record of the place of deposit."

"But how did you proceed ? ".

"I held the vellum again to the fire, after increasing
the heat; but nothing appeared. I now thought it possible that the coating of dirt might have something to
do with the failure; so I carefully rinsed the parchment
by pouring warm water over it, and, having done this, I

placed it in a tin pan, with the skull downwards, and put the pan upon a furnace of lighted charcoal. In a few minutes, the pan having become thoroughly heated, I removed the slip, and, to my inexpressible joy, found it spotted, in several places, with what appeared to be figures arranged in lines. Again I placed it in the pan, and suffered it to remain another minute. Upon taking it off, the whole was just as you see it now."

Here Legrand, having re-heated the parchment, submitted it to my inspection. The following characters were rudely traced, in a red tint, between the death's-head and the goat: —

53‡‡†305))6*;4826)4‡.)4‡);806*;48†8¶60))85;1‡(;:‡*8†83
(88)5*†;46(;88*96*?;8)*‡(;485);5*†2:*‡(;4956*2(5*—4)8¶8*
;4069285);)6†8)4‡‡;1(‡9;48081;8:8‡1;48†85;4)485†528806*
81(‡9;48;(88;4(‡?34;48)4‡;161;:188;‡?;

"But," said I, returning him the slip, "I am as much in the dark as ever. Were all the jewels of Golconda awaiting me upon my solution of this enigma, I am quite sure that I should be unable to earn them."

"And yet," said Legrand, "the solution is by no means so difficult as you might be led to imagine from the first hasty inspection of the characters. These characters, as any one might readily guess, form a cipher, — that is to say, they convey a meaning; but then, from what is known of Kidd, I could not suppose him capable of constructing any of the more abstruse cryptographs. I made up my mind, at once, that this was of a simple species, — such, however, as would appear, to the crude intellect of the sailor, absolutely insoluble without the key."

" And you really solved it ? "

" Readily ; I have solved others of an abstruseness ten thousand times greater. Circumstances, and a certain bias of mind, have led me to take interest in such riddles, and it may well be doubted whether human ingenuity can construct an enigma of the kind which human ingenuity may not, by proper application, resolve. In fact, having once established connected and legible characters, I scarcely gave a thought to the mere difficulty of developing their import.

" In the present case — indeed in all cases of secret writing — the first question regards the *language* of the cipher; for the principles of solution, so far, especially, as the more simple ciphers are concerned, depend upon, and are varied by, the genius of the particular idiom. In general, there is no alternative but experiment (directed by probabilities), of every tongue known to him who attempts the solution, until the true one be attained. But, with the cipher now before us, all difficulty was removed by the signature. The pun upon the word ' Kidd ' is appreciable in no other language than the English. But for this consideration I should have begun my attempts with the Spanish and French, as the tongues in which a secret of this kind would most naturally have been written by a pirate of the Spanish main. As it was, I assumed the cryptograph to be English.

" You observe there are no divisions between the words. Had there been divisions, the task would have been comparatively easy. In such case I should have commenced with a collation and analysis of the shorter words, and, had a word of a single letter occurred, as is most likely (*a* or *I*, for example), I should have considered the solution as assured. But, there being no division, my first step was to ascertain the predominant letters, as well as the least frequent. Counting all, I constructed a table, thus:

Of the character 8 there are 33.

;	"	26.
4	"	19.
‡)	"	16.
*	"	13.
5	"	12.
6	"	11.
† 1	"	8.
0	"	6.
9 2	"	5.
: 3	"	4.
?	"	3.
¶	"	2.
— .	"	1.

"Now, in English, the letter which most frequently occurs is *e*. Afterwards, the succession runs thus: *a o i d h n r s t u y c f g l m w b k p q x z*. *E* predominates so remarkably that an individual sentence of any length is rarely seen, in which it is not the prevailing character.

"Here, then, we have, in the very beginning, the groundwork for something more than a mere guess. The general use which may be made of the table is obvious; but, in this particular cipher, we shall only very partially require its aid. As our predominant character is 8, we will commence by assuming it as the *e* of the natural alphabet. To verify the supposition, let us observe if the 8 be seen often in couples, — for *e* is doubled with great frequency in English, — in such words, for example, as 'meet,' 'fleet,' 'speed,' 'seen,' 'been,' 'agree,' etc. In the present instance we see it doubled no less than five times, although the cryptograph is brief.

"Let us assume 8, then, as *e*. Now, of all *words* in the language, 'the' is most usual; let us see, therefore, whether there are not repetitions of any three characters, in the same order of collocation, the last of them being 8. If we discover repetitions of such letters, so arranged, they will most probably represent the word 'the.' Upon inspection, we find no less than seven such arrangements, the characters being ;48. We may, therefore, assume that ; represents *t*, 4 represents *h*, and 8 represents *e*, — the last being now well confirmed. Thus a great step has been taken.

"But, having established a single word, we are enabled to establish a vastly important point; that is to say, several commencements and terminations of other words. Let us refer, for example, to the last instance but one, in which the combination ;48 occurs, — not far from the end of the cipher. We know that the ; immediately ensuing is the commencement of a word, and, of the six characters succeeding this 'the,' we are cognizant of no less than five. Let us set these characters down, thus, by the letters we know them to represent, leaving a space for the unknown —

t eeth.

"Here we are enabled, at once, to discard the '*th*,' as forming no portion of the word commencing with the first *t*; since, by experiment of the entire alphabet for

a letter adapted to the vacancy, we perceive that no word
can be formed of which this *th* can be a part. We are
thus narrowed into

t ee,

and, going through the alphabet, if necessary, as before,
we arrive at the word ' tree,' as the sole possible reading.
We thus gain another letter, *r*, represented by (, with
the words ' the tree ' in juxtaposition.

"Looking beyond these words, for a short distance,
we again see the combination ;48, and employ it by way
of *termination* to what immediately precedes. We have
thus this arrangement : —

the tree ;4(‡?34 the,

or, substituting the natural letters, where known, it reads
thus : —

the tree thr‡?3h the.

"Now, if, in place of the unknown characters, we
leave blank spaces, or substitute dots, we read thus : —

the tree thr...h the,

when the word ' *through* ' makes itself evident at once.
But this discovery gives us three new letters, *o*, *u*, and *g*,
represented by ‡ ? and 3.

"Looking, now, narrowly, through the cipher for com-
binations of known characters, we find, not very far from
the beginning, this arrangement,

83(88, or egree,

which, plainly, is the conclusion of the word ' degree,' and
gives us another letter, *d*, represented by †.

"Four letters beyond the word 'degree,' we perceive
the combination

;46(;88*.

"Translating the known characters, and representing
the unknown by dots, as before, we read thus : —

th.rtee.,

an arrangement immediately suggestive of the word
'thirteen,' and again furnishing us with two new characters, *i* and *n*, represented by 6 and *.

"Referring, now, to the beginning of the cryptograph,
we find the combination,

53‡‡†.

"Translating, as before, we obtain

.good,

which assures us that the first letter is *A*, and that the
first two words are 'A good.'

"It is now time that we arrange our key, as far as
discovered, in a tabular form, to avoid confusion. It
will stand thus : —

5	represents	a
†	"	d
8	"	e
3	"	g
4	"	h
6	"	i
*	"	n
‡	"	o
(	"	r
;	"	t

"We have, therefore, no less than ten of the most important letters represented, and it will be unnecessary to proceed with the details of the solution. I have said enough to convince you that ciphers of this nature are readily soluble, and to give you some insight into the *rationale* of their development. But be assured that the specimen before us appertains to the very simplest species of cryptograph. It now only remains to give you the full translation of the characters upon the parchment, as unriddled. Here it is : —

" ' *A good glass in the bishop's hostel in the devil's seat forty-one degrees and thirteen minutes northeast and by north main branch seventh limb east side shoot from the left eye of the death's-head a bee line from the tree through the shot fifty feet out.*' "

"But," said I, "the enigma seems still in as bad a condition as ever. How is it possible to extort a meaning from all this jargon about 'devil's seats,' 'death's-heads,' and 'bishop's hotels' ? "

"I confess," replied Legrand, "that the matter still wears a serious aspect, when regarded with a casual glance. My first endeavor was to divide the sentence into the natural division intended by the cryptographist."

"You mean, to punctuate it ? "

"Something of that kind."

"But how was it possible to effect this ? "

"I reflected that it had been a *point* with the writer to run his words together without division, so as to increase the difficulty of solution. Now, a not over-acute man, in pursuing such an object, would be nearly certain

to overdo the matter. When, in the course of his com-
position, he arrived at a break in his subject which
would naturally require a pause, or a point, he would
be exceedingly apt to run his characters, at this place,
more than usually close together. If you will observe
the manuscript in the present instance, you will easily
detect five such cases of unusual crowding. Acting
upon this hint, I made the division thus: —

"'*A good glass in the Bishop's hostel in the Devil's seat
— forty-one degrees and thirteen minutes — northeast and
by north — main branch seventh limb east side — shoot
from the left eye of the death's-head — a bee-line from
the tree through the shot fifty feet out.*'"

"Even this division," said I, "leaves me still in the
dark."

"It left me also in the dark," replied Legrand, "for
a few days; during which I made diligent inquiry, in
the neighborhood of Sullivan's Island, for any building
which went by the name of the 'Bishop's Hotel'; for,
of course, I dropped the obsolete word 'hostel.' Gain-
ing no information on the subject, I was on the point of
extending my sphere of search, and proceeding in a more
systematic manner, when, one morning, it entered into
my head, quite suddenly, that this 'Bishop's Hostel'
might have some reference to an old family, of the name
of Bessop, which, time out of mind, had held possession
of an ancient manor-house, about four miles to the northward of the island. I accordingly went over to the
plantation, and reinstituted my inquiries among the
older negroes of the place. At length one of the most

aged of the women said that she had heard of such a
place as *Bessop's Castle*, and thought that she could
guide me to it, but that it was not a castle, nor a tavern,
but a high rock.

"I offered to pay her well for her trouble, and, after
some demur, she consented to accompany me to the
spot. We found it without much difficulty, when, dis-
missing her, I proceeded to examine the place. The
'castle' consisted of an irregular assemblage of cliffs and
rocks, — one of the latter being quite remarkable for
its height as well as for its insulated and artificial appearance. I clambered to its apex, and then felt much
at a loss as to what should be next done.

"While I was busied in reflection, my eyes fell upon
a narrow ledge in the eastern face of the rock, perhaps
a yard below the summit upon which I stood. This
ledge projected about eighteen inches, and was not more
than a foot wide, while a niche in the cliff just above it
gave it a rude resemblance to one of the hollow-backed
chairs used by our ancestors. I made no doubt that
here was the 'devil's-seat' alluded to in the manuscript,
and now I seemed to grasp the full secret.

"The 'good glass,' I knew, could have reference to
nothing but a telescope; for the word 'glass' is rarely
employed in any other sense by seamen. Now here, I
at once saw, was a telescope to be used, and a definite
point of view, *admitting no variation*, from which to use
it. Nor did I hesitate to believe that the phrases, 'forty-one degrees and thirteen minutes,' and 'northeast and
by north,' were intended as directions for the levelling of
the glass. Greatly excited by these discoveries, I hur-

ried home, procured a telescope, and returned to the rock.

"I let myself down to the ledge, and found that it was impossible to retain a seat upon it except in one particular position. This fact confirmed my preconceived idea. I proceeded to use the glass. Of course, the 'forty-one degrees and thirteen minutes' could allude to nothing but elevation above the visible horizon, since the horizontal direction was clearly indicated by the words, 'northeast and by north.' This latter direction I at once established by means of a pocket-compass; then, pointing the glass as nearly at an angle of forty-one degrees of elevation as I could do it by guess, I moved it cautiously up or down, until my attention was arrested by a circular rift or opening in the foliage of a large tree that overtopped its fellows in the distance. In the centre of this rift I perceived a white spot, but could not, at first, distinguish what it was. Adjusting the focus of the telescope, I again looked, and now made it out to be a human skull.

"Upon this discovery I was so sanguine as to consider the enigma solved; for the phrase, 'main branch, seventh limb, east side,' could refer only to the position of the skull upon the tree, while 'shoot from the left eye of the death's-head' admitted, also, of but one interpretation, in regard to a search for buried treasure. I perceived that the design was to drop a bullet from the left eye of the skull, and that a bee-line, or, in other words, a straight line, drawn from the nearest point of the trunk through 'the shot' (or the spot where the bullet fell), and thence extended to a distance of fifty feet,

would indicate a definite point, — and beneath this point
I thought it at least *possible* that a deposit of value lay
concealed."

"All this," I said, "is exceedingly clear, and, although ingenious, still simple and explicit. When you
left the Bishop's Hotel, what then?"

"Why, having carefully taken the bearings of the tree,
I turned homewards. The instant that I left 'the devil's seat,' however, the circular rift vanished; nor could
I get a glimpse of it afterwards, turn as I would. What
seems to me the chief ingenuity in this whole business
is the fact (for repeated experiment has convinced me it
is a fact) that the circular opening in question is visible
from no other attainable point of view than that afforded
by the narrow ledge upon the face of the rock.

"In this expedition to the 'Bishop's Hotel' I had
been attended by Jupiter, who had, no doubt, observed,
for some weeks past, the abstraction of my demeanor,
and took especial care not to leave me alone. But, on
the next day, getting up very early, I contrived to give
him the slip, and went into the hills in search of the
tree. After much toil I found it. When I came home
at night my valet proposed to give me a flogging. With
the rest of the adventure I believe you are as well acquainted as myself."

"I suppose," said I, "you missed the spot, in the
first attempt at digging, through Jupiter's stupidity in
letting the bug fall through the right instead of through
the left eye of the skull."

"Precisely. This mistake made a difference of about
two inches and a half in the 'shot', — that is to say, in

the position of the peg nearest the tree; and had the treasure been *beneath* the 'shot,' the error would have been of little moment; but 'the shot,' together with the nearest point of the tree, were merely two points for the establishment of a line of direction; of course the error, however trivial in the beginning, increased as we proceeded with the line, and by the time we had gone fifty feet threw us quite off the scent. But for my deep=seated impressions that treasure was here somewhere actually buried, we might have had all our labor in vain."

"But your grandiloquence, and your conduct in swinging the beetle, — how excessively odd! I was sure you were mad. And why did you insist upon letting fall the bug, instead of a bullet, from the skull?"

"Why, to be frank, I felt somewhat annoyed by your evident suspicions touching my sanity, and so resolved to punish you quietly, in my own way, by a little bit of sober mystification. For this reason I swung the beetle, and for this reason I let it fall from the tree. An observation of yours about its great weight suggested the latter idea."

"Yes, I perceive; and now there is only one point which puzzles me. What are we to make of the skeletons found in the hole?"

"That is a question I am no more able to answer than yourself. There seems, however, only one plausible way of accounting for them, — and yet it is dreadful to believe in such atrocity as my suggestion would imply. It is clear that Kidd, — if Kidd indeed secreted this treasure, which I doubt not, — it is clear that he must have had assistance in the labor. But, this labor concluded, he may have thought it expedient to remove all participants in his secret. Perhaps a couple of blows with a mattock were sufficient, while his coadjutors were busy in the pit; perhaps it required a dozen, — who shall tell?"

THE FAIRY-FINDER.

BY SAMUEL LOVER.

INDING a fortune," is a phrase often heard
amongst the peasantry of Ireland. If any man
from small beginnings arrives at wealth, in a
reasonable course of time, the fact is scarcely ever considered as the result of perseverance, superior intelligence, or industry; it passes as a byword through the
country that "he found a fortin"; whether by digging
up a "crock o' goold" in the ruins of an old abbey, or
by catching a Leprechaun and forcing him to "deliver
or die," or discovering it behind an old wainscot, is
quite immaterial: the *when* or *where* is equally unim-
portant, and the thousand are satisfied with the rumor,
"He found a fortin." Besides, going into particulars
destroys romance, — and the Irish are essentially roman-
tic, — and their love of wonder is more gratified in considering the change from poverty to wealth as the result
of superhuman aid, than in attributing it to the mere
mortal causes of industry and prudence.

The crone of every village has plenty of stories to
make her hearers wonder, how fortunes have been

arrived at by extraordinary short cuts; and as it has been laid down as an axiom, "That there never was a fool who had not a greater fool to admire him," so there never was any old woman who told such stories without plenty of listeners.

Now, Darby Kelleher was one of the latter class, and there was a certain collioch * who was an extensive dealer in the marvellous, and could supply "wholesale, retail, and for exportation" any customer such as Darby Kelleher, who not only was a devoted listener, but also made an occasional offering at the cave of the sibyl, in return for her oracular communications. This tribute generally was tobacco, as the collioch was partial to chewing the weed; and thus Darby returned a *quid pro quo*, without having any idea that he was giving a practical instance of the foregoing well-known pun.

Another constant attendant at the hut of the hag was Oonah Lenehan, equally prone to the marvellous with Darby Kelleher, and quite his equal in idleness. A day never passed without Darby and Oonah paying the old woman a visit. She was sure to be "at home," for age and decrepitude rendered it impossible for her to be otherwise; the utmost limit of her ramble from her own chimney-corner being the seat of sods outside the door of her hut, where, in the summer time, she was to be found, so soon as the sunbeams fell on the front of her abode, and made the seat habitable for one whose accustomed vicinity to the fire rendered heat indispensable

* Old woman.

to comfort.   Here she would sit and rock herself to and
fro in the hot noons of July and August, her own appearance and that of her wretched cabin being in admi-
rable keeping.   To a fanciful beholder the question
might have suggested itself, whether the hag was made
for the hovel, or it for her ; or whether they had grown
into a likeness of one another, as man and wife are said
to do, for there were many points of resemblance between them.   The tattered thatch of the hut was like
the straggling hair of its mistress, and Time, that had
grizzled the latter, had covered the former with gray
lichens.   To its mud walls, a strong likeness was to be
found in the tint of the old woman's shrivelled skin ;
they were both seriously out of the perpendicular ; and
the rude mud and wicker chimney of the edifice having
toppled over the gable, stuck out, something in the
fashion of the doodeen, or short pipe, that projected from
the old woman's upper story ; and so they both were
smoking away from morning till night ; and to complete
the similitude sadly, both were poor, — both lonely, —
both fast falling to decay.

Here were Darby Kelleher and Oonah Lenehan sure
to meet every day.   Darby might make his appearance
thus : —

"Good morrow, kindly, granny."

"The same to you, avick," mumbled out the crone.

"Here's some baccy for you, granny."

"Many thanks to you, Darby.   I did n't lay it out
for seeing you so airly, the day."

"No, nor you would n't neither, only I was passin'
this a way, runnin' an arrand for the squire, and I

thought I might as well step in and ax you how you wor."

" Good boy, Darby."

" Throth an' it 's a hot day that 's in it, this blessed day. Phew! Faix, it 's out o' breath I am, and mighty hot intirely; for I was runnin' a'most half the way, bekase it 's an arrand, you see, and the squire towld me to make haste, and so I did, and wint acrass the fields by the short cut; and as I was passin' by the owld castle, I remembered what you towld me awhile agon, granny, about the crock o' goold that is there *for sartin,* if any one could come upon it."

" An' that 's thrue indeed, Darby, avick, — and never heerd any other the longest day I can remember."

" Well, well! think o' that!! O, then it 's he that 'll be the lucky fellow that finds it."

" Thrue for you, Darby ; but that won't be *antil it is laid out* for some one to rise it."

" Sure, that 's what I say to myself often; and why might n't it be my chance to be the man that it was laid out for to find it ? "

" There 's no knowin'," mumbled the crone, mysteriously, as she shook the ashes out of her tobacco-pipe, and replenished the *doodeen* with some of the fresh stock Darby had presented.

" Faix, an' that 's thrue, sure enough. O, but you 've a power o' knowledge, granny!! Sure enough, indeed, there 's no knowin'; but they say there 's great virtue in dhrames."

" That 's ondeniable, Darby," said the hag, " and by the same token maybe you 'd step into the house and bring me out a bit o' 'live turf * to light my pipe."

"To be sure, granny." And away went Darby to execute the commission.

While he was raking, from amongst the embers on the hearth, a piece of turf sufficiently "alive" for the purpose, Oonah made her appearance outside the hut, and gave the usual cordial salutation to the old woman; just as she had done her civility, out came Darby, holding the bit of turf between the two extremities of an osier twig, bent double for the purpose of forming rustic tongs.

"Musha, an' is that you, Darby?" said Oonah.

"Who else would it be?" said Darby.

"Why, you towld me over an hour agone, down there in the big field, that you wor in a hurry."

"And so I am in a hurry, and would n't be here, only I jist stepped in to say God save you to the mother here, and to light her pipe for her, the craythur."

"Well, don't be standin' there, lettin' the coal go black out, Darby," said the woman; "but let me light my pipe at wanst."

"To be sure, granny," said Darby, applying the morsel of lighted ember to the bowl of her pipe, until the process of ignition had been effected. "And now, Oonah, my darlint, if you're so sharp an other people, what the dickens brings you here, when it is mindin'

* In Ireland the tobacco in a pipe is very generally ignited by the application of a piece of burning turf, or, as it is figuratively called, 'live turf.

the geese in the stubbles you ought to be, and not here? What would the misthriss say to that, I wondher?"

"O, I left them safe enough, and they're able to take care of themselves for a bit, and I wanted to ax the granny about a dhrame I had."

"Sure, so do I," said Darby; "and you know *first come first sarved* is a good owld sayin'. And so, granny, you own to it that there's a power o' vartue in dhrames?"

A long-drawn whiff of the pipe was all the hag vouchsafed in return.

"O, then, but that's the iligant tabaccy! musha but it's fine and sthrong, and takes the breath from one a'most, it's so good. Long life to you Darby, — paugh!!"

"You're kindly welkim, granny. An' as I was sayin' about the dhrames, — you say there's a power o' vartue in them."

"Who says agin it?" said the hag, authoritatively, and looking with severity on Darby.

"Sure, an' it's not me you'd suspect o' the like? I was only goin' to say that *myself* had a mighty sharp dhrame last night, and sure I kem to ax you about the maynin' av it."

"Well, avic, tell us your dhrame," said the hag, sucking her pipe with increased energy.

"Well, you see," said Darby, "I dhremt I was goin' along a road, and that all of a suddint I kem to *crass* roads, and you know there's great vartue in crass roads."

"That's thrue, avourneen! — paugh!! — go an."

"Well, as I was sayin', I kem to the crass roads, and

soon afther I seen four walls; now I think the four walls *manes* the owld castle."

"Likely enough, avic."

"O," said Oonah, who was listening with her mouth as wide open as if the faculty of hearing lay there, instead of in her ears, "sure, you know the owld castle has only *three* walls, and how could that be it ? "

"No matther for that," said the crone, "it *ought* to have four, and that 's the same thing."

"Well! well! I never thought o' that," said Oonah, lifting her hands in wonder; "sure enough, so it ought ! "

"Go an, Darby," said the hag.

"Well, I thought the greatest sight o' crows ever I seen flew out o' the castle, and I think *that* must mane the goold there is in it."

"Did you count how many there was ? " said the hag, with great solemnity.

"Faith, I never thought o' that," said Darby, with an air of vexation.

"Could you tell me, itself, wor they odd or even, avic ? "

"Faix, an' I could not say for *sartin*."

"Ah, that 's it!! " said the crone, shaking her head in token of disappointment. "How can I tell the maynin' o' your dhrame, if you don't know how it kem out exactly ? "

"Well, granny, but don't you think the crows was *likely* for goold ? "

"Yis, — if they flew heavy."

"Throth, then, an' now I remimber they did fly

heavy, and I said to myself there would be rain soon, the crows was flyin' so heavy."

"I wish you did n't dhrame o' rain, Darby."

"Why, granny? What harm is it?"

"O, nothin', only it comes in a crass place there."

"But it does n't spile the dhrame, I hope?"

"O no. Go an."

"Well, with that, I thought I was passin' by Doolins the miller's, and says he to me, 'Will you carry home this sack o' male for me?' Now, you know, male is money, every fool knows!"

"Right, avic."

"And so I tuk the sack o' male an my shouldher, and I thought the woight iv it was killin' me, just as if it *was* a sack o' goold."

"Go an, Darby."

"And with that I thought I met with a cat, and that, you know, manes an ill-nathur'd woman."

"Right, Darby."

"And says she to me, 'Darby Kelleher,' says she, 'you 're mighty yollow, God bless you; is it the jandhers you have?' says she. Now was n't that mighty sharp? I think the jandhers manes goold?"

"Yis, iv it was the yollow jandhers you dhremt iv, and not the black jandhers."

"Well, it *was* the yollow jandhers."

"Very good, avic; that 's makin' a fair offer at it."

"I thought so, myself," said Darby, "more by token when there was a dog in my dhrame next; and that 's a frind, you know."

"Right, avic."

E

"And he had a silver collar an him."

"O, bad luck to that silver collar, Darby; what made you dhrame o' silver at all?"

"Why, what harm?"

"O, I thought you knew bether nor to dhrame o' silver; why, cushla machree, sure silver is a disappointment all the world over."

"O murther!" said Darby, in horror, "and is my dhrame spylte by that blackguard collar?"

"Nigh hand indeed, but not all out. It would be spylte only for the dog, but the dog is a frind, and so it will be only a frindly disappointment, or maybe a fallin' out with an acquaintance."

"O, what matther," said Darby, "so the dhrame is to the good still!!"

"The dhrame *is* to the good still; but tell me if you dhremt o' three sprigs o' *spare*mint at the ind iv it?"

"Why, then, now I could not say for sartin, bekase I was nigh wakin' at the time, and the dhrame was not so clear to me."

"I wish you could be sartin o' that."

"Why, I have it an my mind that there *was* sparemint in it, bekase I thought there was a garden in part iv it, and the sparemint was *likely* to be there."

"Sure enough, and so you did dhrame o' the three sprigs o' sparemint?"

"Indeed, I could a'most make my book-oath that I dhremt iv it. I 'm partly sartin, if not all out."

"Well, that 's raysonable. It 's a good dhrame, Darby."

"Do you tell me so!"

" 'Deed an' it is, Darby. Now wait till the next quar-ther o' the new moon, and dhrame again *then*, and you 'll see what 'll come of it."

"By dad an' I will, granny. O but it 's you *has* taken the maynin' out of it beyant everything; and faix if I find the crock, it 's yourself won't be the worse iv it; but I must be goin', granny, for the squire bid me to hurry, or else I would stay longer wid you. Good mornin' to you — good mornin', Oonah! I 'll see you to-morrow some time, granny." And off went Darby, leisurely enough.

The foregoing dialogue shows the ready credulity of poor Darby; but it was not in his belief of the "vartue of dhrames" that his weakness only lay. He likewise had a most extensive creed as regarded fairies of all sorts and sizes, and was always on the lookout for a Lepre-chaun. Now a Leprechaun is a fairy of peculiar tastes, properties, and powers, which it is necessary to acquaint the reader with. His taste as to occupation is very humble, for he employs himself in making shoes, and he loves retirement, being fond of shady nooks where he can sit alone and pursue his avocation undisturbed. He is quite a hermit in this respect, for there is no instance on record of two Leprechauns being seen together. But he is quite a beau in his dress, notwithstanding, for he wears a red square-cut coat, richly laced with gold, waistcoat and inexpressibles of the same, cocked hat, shoes, and buckles. He has the property of deceiving, in so great a degree, those who chance to discover him, that none have ever yet been known whom he has not overreached in the "keen encounter of the wits," which his meeting with mortals always produces. This is occasioned by his possessing the power of bestowing unbounded wealth on whoever can keep him within sight until he is weary of the *surveillance,* and gives the ransom demanded, and to this end, the object of the mortal who is so fortunate as to surprise one is to seize him and never withdraw his eye from him, until the threat of destruction forces the Leprechaun to produce the treasure; but the sprite is too many for us clumsy-witted earthlings, and is sure, by some device, to make us avert our eyes, when he vanishes at once.

This Enchanted Cobbler of the meadows, Darby Kelleher was always on the lookout for. But though so constantly on the watch for a Leprechaun, he never had got even within sight of one, and the name of the Fairy-Finder was bestowed upon him in derision. Many a trick too was played upon him; sometimes a twig stuck amongst long grass, with a red rag hanging upon it, has betrayed Darby into a cautious observance and approach, until a nearer inspection, and a laugh from behind some neighboring hedge, have dispelled the illusion. But this, though often repeated, did not cure him, and no turkeycock had a quicker eye for a bit of red, or flew at it with greater eagerness, than Darby Kelleher; and he entertained the belief that one day or other he would reap the reward of all his watching, by finding a Leprechaun in good earnest.

But that was all in the hands of Fate, and must be waited for; in the mean time there was the castle and the "crock o' goold" for a certainty, and, under the good omens of the "sharp dhrame" he had, he determined on taking that affair in hand at once. For his companion in the labor of digging, and pulling the ponderous walls of the castle to pieces, he selected Oonah, who was, in the parlance of her own class, "a brave two-handed long-sided jack," and as great a believer in dreams and omens as Darby himself; besides, she promised profound secrecy, and agreed to take a small share of the treasure for her reward in assisting to discover it.

For about two months Darby and Oonah labored in vain; but at last something came of their exertions. In the course of their work, when they occasionally got tired, they would sit down to rest themselves and talk over their past disappointments and future hopes. Now it was during one of these intervals of repose that Darby, as he was resting himself on one of the coign-stones of the ruin, suddenly discovered — that he was in love with Oonah.

Now Oonah happened to be thinking much in the same sort of way about Darby, at that very moment, and the end of the affair was, that Darby and Oonah were married the Sunday following.

The calculating Englishman will ask, Did he find the treasure before he married the girl? The unsophisticated boys of the sod never calculate on these occasions; and the story goes that Oonah Lenehan was the only treasure Darby discovered in the old castle. Darby's acquaintances were in high glee on the occasion, and swore he got *a great lob;* for Oonah, be it remembered, was on the grenadier scale, or what in Ireland is called "the full of a door," and the news spread over the country in some such fashion as this: —

"Arrah, an' did you hear the news?"

"What news?"

"About Darby Kelleher."

"What of him?"

"Sure he found a fairy at last."

"Tare an ounty!"

"Thruth I'm tellin' you. He's married to Oonah Lenehan."

"Ha! ha! ha! by the powers it's she that is the rale fairy! musha, more power to you, Darby, but you 've cotched it in airnest now!"

But the fairy he had caught did not satisfy Darby so far as to make him give up the pursuit for the future. He was still on the watch for a Leprechaun; and one morning, as he was going to his work, he stopped suddenly on his path, which lay through a field of standing corn, and his eye became riveted on some object with the most eager expression. He crouched, and crawled, and was making his way with great caution towards the point of his attraction, when he was visited on the back of the head with a thump that considerably disturbed his visual powers, and the voice of his mother, a vigorous old beldame, saluted his ear at the same time with a hearty, "Bad luck to you, you lazy thief, what are you slindging there for, when it's minding your work you ought to be?"

"Whisht! whisht! mother," said Darby, holding up his hand in token of silence.

"What do you mane, you omadhaun?"

"Mother, be quiet, I bid you! whisht! I see it!"

"What do you see?"

"Stoop down here. Straight forninst you, don't you see it as plain as a pikestaff?"

"See what?"

"That little red thing."

"Well, what of it?"

"See there, how it stirs. O murther! it's goin' to be off afore I can catch it. O murther! why did you come here at all, makin' a noise and frightenin' it away?"

"Frightenin' what, you big fool?"

"The Leprechaun there. Whisht! it is quiet agin!"

"May the d——l run a huntin' wid you for a big omad-haun; why, you born nath'ral, is it that red thing over there you mane?"

"Yis, to be sure it is; don't spake so loud, I tell you."

"Why, bad scran to you, you fool, it's a poppy it is, and nothin' else." And the old woman went over to the spot where it grew, and plucking it up by the roots threw it at Darby, with a great deal of abuse into the bargain, and bade him go mind his work, instead of being a "slindging vagabóne, as he was."

It was some time after this occurrence, that Darby Kelleher had a meeting with a certain Doctor Dionysius Mac Finn, whose name became much more famous than it had hitherto been, from the wonderful events that ensued in consequence.

Of the doctor himself it becomes necessary to say something. His father was one Paddy Finn, and had been so prosperous in the capacity of a cow doctor, that his son Denis, seeing the dignity of a professor in the

healing art must increase in proportion to the nobleness
of the animal he operates upon, determined to make the
human, instead of the brute creation, the object of his
care. To this end he was assisted by his father, who
had scraped some money together in his humble calling,
and having a spice of ambition in him, as well as his
aspiring son, he set him up in the neighboring village as
an apothecary. Here Denny enjoyed the reputation of
being an "iligant bone-setter," and cracked skulls, the
result of *fair* fighting, and whiskey fevers were treated
by him on the most approved principles. But Denny's
father was gathered unto *his* fathers, and the son came
into the enjoyment of all the old man's money: this,
considering his condition, was considerable, and the possession of a few hundred pounds so inflated the apothecary, that he determined on becoming a "Doctor" at
once. For this purpose he gave up his apothecary's
shop, and set off — where do you think? — to Spain.
Here he remained for some time, and returned to Ireland, declaring himself a full physician of one of the
Spanish universities; his name of Denny Finn trans-
formed into Doctor Dionysius Mac Finn, or, as his
neighbors chose to call it, Mac Fun, and fun enough
the doctor certainly gave birth to. The little money he
once had was spent in his pursuit of professional honors,
and he returned to his native place with a full title and
an empty purse, and his practice did not tend to fill it.
At the same time there was a struggle to keep up ap-
pearances. He kept a horse, or what he intended to be
considered as such, but 't was only a pony, and if he had
but occasion to go to the end of the village on a visit,

the pony was ordered on service. He was glad to accept an invitation to dinner wherever he had the luck to get one, and the offer of a bed, even, was sure to be accepted, because that insured breakfast the next morning. Thus poor Doctor Dionysius made out the cause; often asked to dinner from mingled motives of kindness and fun, for while a good dinner was a welcome novelty to the doctor, the absurdities of his pretension and manner rendered him a subject of unfailing diversion to his entertainers. Now he had gone the round of all the snug farmers and country gentlemen in the district, but at last he had the honor to receive an invitation from *the* squire himself, and on the appointed day Doctor Dionysius bestrode his pony, attired in the full dress of a Spanish physician, which happens to be *red* from head to foot, and presented himself at "The Hall."

When a groom appeared to take his "horse" to the stable, the doctor requested that his steed might be turned loose into the lawn, declaring it to be more wholesome for the animal than being cooped up in a house; the saddle and bridle were accordingly removed, and his desire complied with.

The doctor's appearance in the drawing-room, attired as he was, caused no small diversion, but attention was speedily called off from him by the announcement of dinner, that electric sound that stimulates a company at the same instant, and supersedes every other consideration whatsoever. Moreover, the squire's dinners were notoriously good, and the doctor profited largely by the same that day, and lost no opportunity of filling his glass with the choice wines that surrounded him. This he did to so much purpose, that the poor little man was very far gone when the guests were about to separate.

At the doctor's request the bell was rung, and his horse ordered, as the last remaining few of the company were about to separate, but every one of them had departed, and still there was no announcement of the steed being at the door. At length a servant made his appearance, and said it was impossible to catch the doctor's pony.

"What do you mean by 'catch'?" said the squire. "Is it not in the stable?"

"No, sir."

Here an explanation ensued, and the squire ordered a fresh attempt to be made to take the fugitive; but, though many fresh hands were employed in the attempt, the pony baffled all their efforts; every manœuvre usually resorted to on such occasions, was vainly put in practice. He was screwed up into corners, but no sooner was he there than, squealing and flinging up his heels, he broke through the blockade; — again his flank was turned by nimble runners, but the pony was nimbler still; a sieve full of oats was presented as an inducement, but the pony was above such vulgar tricks, and defied all attempts at being captured.

This was the mode by which the doctor generally secured the offer of a bed, and he might have been successful in this instance, but for a knowing old coachman who was up to the trick, and out of pure fun chose to expose it; so, bringing out a huge blunderbuss, he said, "Never mind, — just let me at him, and I'll engage I'll make him stand."

"O my good man," said the doctor, "pray don't take so much trouble; just let me go with you." And proceeding to the spot where the pony was still luxuriating on the rich grass of the squire's lawn, he gave a low whistle, and the little animal walked up to his owner with as much tractability as a dog. The saddling and bridling did not take much time, and the doctor was obliged to renounce his hopes of a bed and to-morrow's breakfast, and ride home, — or homewards, I should say, for it was as little his destiny as his wish to sleep at home that night: for he was so overpowered with his potations, that he could not guide the pony, and the pony's palate was so tickled by the fresh herbage, that he wished for more of it, and finding a gate that led to a meadow open by the roadside, he turned into the field, where he very soon turned the doctor into a ditch, so that they had bed and board between them to their heart's content.

The doctor and his horse slept and ate profoundly all night, and even the "rosy-fingered morn," as the poets have it, found them in the continuance of their enjoyment. Now it happened that Darby Kelleher was passing along the path that lay by the side of the ditch where the doctor was sleeping, and on perceiving him, Darby made as dead a set as ever pointer did at game.

The doctor, be it remembered, was dressed in red. Moreover, he was a little man, and his gold-laced hat and ponderous shoe-buckles completed the resemblance to the being that Darby took him for. Darby was at last certain that he had discovered a Leprechaun, and amaze so riveted him to the spot, and anxiety made his

pulse beat so fast, that he could not move nor breathe for
some seconds. At last he recovered himself, and going stealthily to the spot where the doctor slept, every
inch of his approach made him more certain of the reality of his prize ; and when he found himself within reach
of it, he made one furious spring, and flung himself on
the unfortunate little man, fastening his tremendous fist
on his throat, at the same time exclaiming in triumph,
"Hurra! — by the hoky, I have you at last ! ! "

The poor little doctor, thus rudely and suddenly
aroused from his tipsy sleep, looked excessively bewildered when he opened his eyes, and met the glare of
ferocious delight that Darby Kelleher cast upon him, and
he gurgled out, "What 's the matter ? " as well as the
grip of Darby's hand upon his throat would permit him.

"Goold 's the matther," shouted Darby, — "Goold !
— Goold ! ! — Goold ! ! ! "

"What about Goold ? " says the doctor.

"Goold ! — yellow goold — that 's the matther."

"Is it Paddy Goold that 's taken ill again ? " said the
doctor, rubbing his eyes. "Don't choke me, my good
man; I 'll go immediately," said he, endeavoring to rise.

"By my sowl, you won't," said Darby, tightening his
hold.

"For mercy's sake let me go ! " said the doctor.

"Let you go indeed ! — ow ! ow ! "

"For the tender mercy — "

"Goold ! goold ! you little vagabone ! "

"Well, I 'm going, if you let me."

"Divil a step." And here he nearly choked him.

"Oh ! murder ! — for God's sake ! "

"Whisht!! — you thief, — how *dar* you say God, you divil's imp!!!"

The poor little man, between the suddenness of his waking and the roughness of the treatment he was under, was in such a state of bewilderment, that for the first time he now perceived he was lying amongst grass and under bushes, and, rolling his eyes about, he exclaimed, —

"Where am I? — God bless me!"

"Whisht! you little cruked ottomy — by the holy farmer, if you say God agin, I'll cut your throat."

"What do you hold me so tight for?"

"Just for fear you'd vanish, you see. O, I know you well!"

"Then, my good man, if you know me so well, treat me with proper respect, if you please."

"Divil send you respect. Respect indeed! that's a good thing. Musha bad luck to your impidence, you thievin' owld rogue."

"Who taught you to call such names to your betters, fellow? How dare you use a professional gentleman so rudely?"

"O, do you hear this!! — a profissionil gintleman! Arrah, do you think I don't know you, you little owld cobbler?"

"Cobbler! Zounds, what do you mean, you ruffian? Let me go, sirrah!" And he struggled violently to rise.

"Not a taste, 'scure to the step you'll go out o' this till you give me what I want."

"What do you want, then?"

"Goold — goold!"

"Ho! ho! so you're a robber, sir; you want to rob me, do you?"

"Oh! what robbery it is!! — throth that won't do, as cunnin' as you think yourself; you won't frighten me that way. Come, give it at wanst, — you may as well. I'll never let go my grip o' you antil you hand me out the goold."

"'Pon the honor of a gentleman, gold nor silver is not in my company. I have fourpence halfpenny in my breeches-pocket, which you are welcome to if you let go my throat."

"Fourpence hapny!!! Why, then, do you think me sitch a *gom*, all out, as to put me off wid fourpence hapny; throth, for three sthraws, this minit I'd thrash you within an inch o' your life for your impidence. Come, no humbuggin'; out with the goold!"

"I have no gold. Don't choke me: if you murder me, remember there's law in the land. You'd better let me go."

"Not a fut. Gi' me the goold, I tell you, you little vagabone!!" said Darby, shaking him violently.

"Don't murder me, for Heaven's sake!"

"I will murdher you if you don't give me a hatful o' goold this minit."

"A hatful of gold! Why, whom do you take me for?"

"Sure I know you're a Leprechaun, you desaiver o' the world!"

"A Leprechaun!" said the doctor, in mingled indignation and amazement. "My good man, you mistake."

"O, how soft I am! 'T won't do, I tell you. I have

you, and I 'll howld you; long I 've been lookin' for you, and I cotch you at last, and by the tarnal o' war I 'll have your life or the goold."

" My good man, be merciful — you mistake — I 'm no Leprechaun; I 'm Doctor Mac Finn."

" That won't do either! you think to desaive me, but 't won't do; — just as if I did n't know a docthor from a Leprechaun. Gi' me the goold, you owld chate!"

" I tell you I 'm Doctor Dionysius Mac Finn. Take care what you 're about! — there 's law in the land; and I think I begin to know you. Your name is Kelleher?"

" O, you cunnin' owld thief! O, then, but you are the complate owld rogue; only I 'm too able for you. You want to freken me, do you? O, you little scrap o' deception, but you are deep!"

" Your name is Kelleher — I remember. My good fellow, take care; don't you know I 'm Doctor Mac Finn, — don't you see I am?"

" Why thin but you have the dirty yollow pinched look iv him, sure enough; but don't I know you 've only put it an you to desaive me; besides, the doctor has dirty owld tatthers o' black clothes an him, and is n't as red as a sojer, like you."

" That 's an accident, my good man."

" Gi' me the goold this minit, and no more prate wid you."

" I tell you, Kelleher — "

" Howld your tongue, and gi' me the goold."

" By all that 's — "

" Will you give it?"

"How can I?"

"Very well. You'll see what the ind of it 'ill be," said Darby, rising, but still keeping his iron grip of the doctor. "Now, for the last time, I ask you, will you gi' me the goold? or, by the powers o' wildfire, I'll put you where you'll never see daylight antil you make me a rich man."

"I have no gold, I tell you."

"Faix, then I'll keep you till you find it," said Darby, who tucked the little man under his arm, and ran home with him as fast as he could.

He kicked at his cabin door for admittance when he reached home, exclaiming, —

"Let me in! let me in! Make haste; I have him."

"Who have you?" said Oonah, as she opened the door.

"Look at that!" said Darby in triumph; "I cotch him at last!"

"Weira then, is it a Leprechaun it is?" said Oonah.

"Divil a less," said Darby, throwing down the doctor on the bed, and still holding him fast. "Open the big chest, Oonah, and we'll lock him up in it, and keep him antil he gives us the goold."

"Murder! murder!" shouted the doctor. "Lock me up in a chest!!"

"Gi' me the goold, then, and I won't."

"My good man, you know I have not gold to give."

"Don't believe him, Darby jewel," said Oonah; "them Leprechauns is the biggest liars in the world."

"Sure I know that!" said Darby, "as well as you. Oh! all the throuble I've had wid him; throth only I'm

aiqual to a counsellor for knowledge, he 'd have nam-
plushed me long ago."

" Long life to you, Darby dear ! "

" Mrs. Kelleher," said the doctor.

" O Lord ! " said Oonah, in surprise, " did you ever
hear the like o' that ? — how he knows my name ! "

"To be sure he does," said Darby, " and why nat ?
sure he 's a fairy, you know."

" I 'm no fairy, Mrs. Kelleher. I 'm a doctor, — Doctor Mac Finn."

" Don't b'lieve him, darlin'," said Darby. " Make
haste and open the chest."

" Darby Kelleher," said the doctor, " let me go, and
I 'll cure you whenever you want my assistance."

"Well, I want your assistance now," said Darby,
" for I 'm very bad this minit wid poverty ; and if you
cure me o' that, I 'll let you go."

" What will become of me ? " said the doctor in
despair, as Darby carried him towards the big chest
which Oonah had opened.

" I 'll tell you what 'll become o' you," said Darby,
seizing a hatchet that lay within his reach ; " by the
seven blessed candles, if you don't consint before night
to fill that big chest full o' goold, I 'll chop you as small
as aribs (herbs) for the pot." And Darby crammed
him into the box.

" O Mrs. Kelleher, be merciful to me," said the doctor, " and whenever you 're sick I 'll attend you."

"God forbid ! " said Oonah ; " it 's not the likes o'
you I want when I 'm sick ; — attind me, indeed ! bad
luck to you, you little imp, maybe you 'd run away with

4 *   F

my babby, or it's a *Banshee* you'd turn yourself into,
and sing for my death. Shut him up, Darby; it's not
looky to be howldin' discoorse wid the likes iv him."

"Oh!" roared the doctor, as his cries were stifled by
the lid of the chest being closed on him. The key was
turned, and Oonah sprinkled some holy water she had
in a little bottle that hung in one corner of the cabin
over the lock, to prevent the fairy having any power
upon it.

Darby and Oonah now sat down in consultation on
their affairs, and began forming their plans on an extensive scale, as to what they were to do with their money,
for have it they must, now that the Leprechaun was
fairly in their power. Now and then Darby would rise
and go over to the chest, very much as one goes to the
door of a room where a naughty child has been locked
up, to know "if it be good yet," and giving a thump
on the lid would exclaim, "Well, you little vagabone,
will you gi' me the goold yet?"

A groan and a faint answer of denial was all the reply
he received.

"Very well, stay there; but, remember, if you don't
consint before night I'll chop you to pieces." He then
got his bill-hook, and began to sharpen it close by the
chest, that the Leprechaun might hear him; and when
the poor doctor heard this process going forward, he felt
more dead than alive; the horrid scraping of the iron
against the stone being interspersed with occasional in-
terjectional passages from Darby, such as, "Do you hear
that, you thief? I'm gettin' ready for you." Then away
he'd rasp at the grindstone again, and, as he paused to

feel the edge of the weapon, exclaim, "By the powers, I 'll have it as sharp as a razhir."

In the mean time it was well for the prisoner that there were many large chinks in the chest, or suffocation from his confinement would have anticipated Darby's pious intentions upon him; and when he found matters likely to go so hard with him, the thought struck him at last of affecting to be what Darby mistook him for, and regaining his freedom by stratagem.

To this end, when Darby had done sharpening his bill-hook, the doctor replied, in answer to one of Darby's summonses for gold, that he saw it was in vain longer to deny giving it, that Darby was too cunning for him, and that he was ready to make him the richest man in the country.

"I 'll take no less than the full o' that chest," said Darby.

"You 'll have ten times the full of it, Darby," said the doctor, "if you 'll only do what I bid you."

"Sure I 'll do anything."

"Well, you must first prepare the mystificand-herum-brandherum."

"Tare an ouns, how do I know what that is?"

"Silence, Darby Kelleher, and attend to me: that 's a magical ointment, which I will show you how to make; and whenever you want gold, all you have to do is to rub a little of it on the point of a pickaxe or your spade, and dig wherever you please, and you will be sure to find treasure."

"O, think o' that! faix, an' I 'll make plenty of it, when you show me. How is it made?"

"You must go into the town, Darby, and get me three
things, and fold them three times in three rags torn out
of the left side of a petticoat that has not known water
for a year."

"Faith, I can do that much, anyhow," said Oonah,
who began tearing the prescribed pieces out of her under-
garment.

"And what three things am I to get you?"

"First bring me a grain of salt from a house that
stands at cross-roads."

"Crass roads!" said Darby, looking significantly at
Oonah. "By my sowl, but it's my dhrame's comin'
out!"

"Silence, Darby Kelleher," said the doctor with great
solemnity; "mark me, Darby Kelleher." And then
he proceeded to repeat a parcel of gibberish to Darby,
which he enjoined him to remember, and repeat again;
but as Darby could not, the doctor said he should only
write it down for him, and, tearing a leaf from his
pocket-book, he wrote in pencil a few words, stating the
condition he was in, and requesting assistance. This
slip of paper he desired Darby to deliver to the apothecary in the town, who would give him a drug that would
complete the making of the ointment.

Darby went to the apothecary's as he was desired, and
it happened to be dinner-time when he arrived. The
apothecary had a few friends dining with him, and Darby
was detained until they chose to leave the table, and go,
in a body, to liberate the poor little doctor. He was
pulled out of the chest amidst the laughter of his liber-
ators and the fury of Darby and Oonah, who both made

considerable fight against being robbed of their prize. At last the doctor's friends got him out of the house, and proceeded to the town to supper, where the whole party kept getting magnificently drunk, until sleep plunged them into dizzy dreams of Leprechauns and Fairy-Finders.

The doctor for some days swore vengeance against Darby, and threatened a prosecution; but his friends recommended him to let the matter rest, as it would only tend to make the affair more public, and get him nothing but laughter for damages.

As for Darby Kelleher, nothing could ever persuade him that it was not a *real* Leprechaun he had caught, which by some villanous contrivance, on the Fairy's part, changed itself into the semblance of the doctor; and he often said the great mistake he made was "givin' the little vagabone so much time, for that if he had done right he'd have set about cutting his throat at wanst."

MURAD THE UNLUCKY.

BY MARIA EDGEWORTH.

I.

IT is well known that the grand seignior amuses himself by going at night, in disguise, through the streets of Constantinople; as the caliph, Haroun Alraschid, used formerly to do in Bagdad.

One moonlight night, accompanied by his grand vizier, he traversed several of the principal streets of the city, without seeing anything remarkable. At length, as they were passing a rope-maker's, the sultan recollected the Arabian story of Cogia-Hassan Alhabal, the rope-maker, and his two friends, Saad and Saadi, who differed so much in their opinion concerning the influence of fortune over human affairs.

"What is your opinion on this subject?" said the grand seignior to his vizier.

"I am inclined, please your majesty," replied the vizier, "to think that success in the world depends more upon prudence than upon what is called luck, or fortune."

"And I," said the sultan, "am persuaded that fortune

does more for men than prudence. Do you not every day hear of persons who are said to be fortunate or unfortunate? How comes it that this opinion should prevail amongst men, if it be not justified by experience?"

"It is not for me to dispute with your majesty," replied the prudent vizier.

"Speak your mind freely; I desire and command it," said the sultan.

"Then I am of opinion," answered the vizier, "that people are often led to believe others fortunate, or unfortunate, merely because they only know the general outline of their histories; and are ignorant of the incidents and events in which they have shown prudence or imprudence. I have heard, for instance, that there are at present in this city two men, who are remarkable for their good and bad fortune: one is called *Murad the Unlucky*, and the other *Saladin the Lucky*. Now I am inclined to think, if we could hear their stories, we should find that one is a prudent and the other an imprudent character."

"Where do these men live?" interrupted the sultan. "I will hear their histories from their own lips, before I sleep."

"Murad the Unlucky lives in the next square," said the vizier.

The sultan desired to go thither immediately. Scarcely had they entered the square, when they heard the cry of loud lamentations. They followed the sound till they came to a house of which the door was open, and where there was a man tearing his turban, and weeping bitterly. They asked the cause of his distress, and he pointed to the fragments of a china vase, which lay on the pavement at his door.

"This seems undoubtedly to be beautiful china," said the sultan, taking up one of the broken pieces; "but can the loss of a china vase be the cause of such violent grief and despair?"

"Ah, gentlemen," said the owner of the vase, suspending his lamentations, and looking at the dress of the pretended merchants, "I see that you are strangers: you do not know how much cause I have for grief and despair! You do not know that you are speaking to Murad the Unlucky! Were you to hear all the unfortunate accidents that have happened to me, from the time I was born till this instant, you would perhaps pity me, and acknowledge I have just cause for despair."

Curiosity was strongly expressed by the sultan; and the hope of obtaining sympathy inclined Murad to gratify it, by the recital of his adventures. "Gentlemen," said he, "I scarcely dare invite you into the house of such an unlucky being as I am; but, if you will venture to take a night's lodging under my roof, you shall hear at your leisure the story of my misfortunes."

The sultan and the vizier excused themselves from spending the night with Murad; saying that they were obliged to proceed to their khan, where they should be expected by their companions: but they begged permission to repose themselves for half an hour in his house, and besought him to relate the history of his life, if it would not renew his grief too much to recollect his misfortunes.

Few men are so miserable as not to like to talk of their misfortunes, where they have, or where they think they have, any chance of obtaining compassion. As soon as the pretended merchants were seated, Murad began his story in the following manner : —

"My father was a merchant of this city. The night before I was born, he dreamed that I came into the world with the head of a dog and the tail of a dragon; and that, in haste to conceal my deformity, he rolled me up in a piece of linen, which unluckily proved to be the grand seignior's turban; who, enraged at his insolence in touching his turban, commanded that his head should be struck off.

"My father awaked before he lost his head, but not before he had lost half his wits from the terror of his dream. He considered it as a warning sent from above, and consequently determined to avoid the sight of me. He would not stay to see whether I should really be born with the head of a dog and the tail of a dragon; but he set out, the next morning, on a voyage to Aleppo.

"He was absent for upwards of seven years; and during that time my education was totally neglected. One day I inquired from my mother why I had been named Murad the Unlucky. She told me that this name was given to me in consequence of my father's dream; but she added that perhaps it might be forgotten, if I proved fortunate in my future life. My nurse, a very old woman, who was present, shook her head, with a look which I shall never forget, and whispered to my mother loud enough for me to hear, ' Unlucky

he was, and is, and ever will be.   Those that are born to
ill luck cannot help themselves; nor can any, but the
great prophet Mahomet himself, do anything for them.
It is a folly for an unlucky person to strive with his
fate : it is better to yield to it at once.'

"This speech made a terrible impression upon me,
young as I then was ; and every accident that happened
to me afterwards confirmed my belief in my nurse's
prognostic.   I was in my eighth year when my father
returned from abroad.   The year after he came home
my brother Saladin was born, who was named Saladin
the Lucky, because the day he was born a vessel
freighted with rich merchandise for my father arrived
safely in port.

"I will not weary you with a relation of all the little
instances of good fortune by which my brother Saladin
was distinguished, even during his childhood.   As he
grew up, his success in everything he undertook was as
remarkable as my ill luck in all that I attempted.   From
the time the rich vessel arrived, we lived in splendor ;
and the supposed prosperous state of my father's affairs
was of course attributed to the influence of my brother
Saladin's happy destiny.

"When Saladin was about twenty, my father was
taken dangerously ill ; and as he felt that he should not
recover, he sent for my brother to the side of his bed,
and, to his great surprise, informed him that the magnificence in which we had lived had exhausted all his
wealth ; that his affairs were in the greatest disorder ;
for, having trusted to the hope of continual success, he
had embarked in projects beyond his powers.

"The sequel was, he had nothing remaining to leave to his children but two large china vases, remarkable for their beauty, but still more valuable on account of certain verses inscribed upon them in an unknown character, which was supposed to operate as a talisman or charm in favor of their possessors.

"Both these vases my father bequeathed to my brother Saladin; declaring he could not venture to leave either of them to me, because I was so unlucky that I should inevitably break it. After his death, however, my brother Saladin, who was blessed with a generous temper, gave me my choice of the two vases; and endeavored to raise my spirits, by repeating frequently that he had no faith either in good fortune or ill fortune.

"I could not be of his opinion, though I felt and acknowledged his kindness in trying to persuade me out of my settled melancholy. I knew it was in vain for me to exert myself, because I was sure that, do what I would, I should still be Murad the Unlucky. My brother, on the contrary, was nowise cast down, even by the poverty in which my father left us: he said he was sure he should find some means of maintaining himself, and so he did.

"On examining our china vases, he found in them a powder of a bright scarlet color; and it occurred to him that it would make a fine dye. He tried it, and after some trouble, it succeeded to admiration.

"During my father's lifetime, my mother had been supplied with rich dresses, by one of the merchants who was employed by the ladies of the grand seignior's seraglio. My brother had done this merchant some trifling favors; and, upon application to him, he readily engaged to recommend the new scarlet dye. Indeed, it was so beautiful, that, the moment it was seen, it was preferred to every other color. Saladin's shop was soon crowded with customers; and his winning manners and pleasant conversation were almost as advantageous to him as his scarlet dye. On the contrary, I observed that the first glance at my melancholy countenance was sufficient to disgust every one who saw me. I perceived this plainly; and it only confirmed me the more in my belief in my own evil destiny.

"It happened one day that a lady, richly apparelled and attended by two female slaves, came to my brother's house to make some purchases. He was out, and I alone was left to attend to the shop. After she had looked over some goods, she chanced to see my china vase, which was in the room. She took a prodigious fancy to it, and offered me any price if I would part with it; but this I declined doing, because I believed that I should draw down upon my head some dreadful calamity, if I voluntarily relinquished the talisman. Irritated by my refusal, the lady, according to the custom of her sex, became more resolute in her purpose; but neither entreaties nor money could change my determination. Provoked beyond measure at my obstinacy, as she called it, she left the house.

"On my brother's return, I related to him what had happened, and expected that he would have praised me for my prudence; but, on the contrary, he blamed me for the superstitious value I set upon the verses on my vase; and observed that it would be the height of folly to lose a certain means of advancing my fortune, for the uncertain hope of magical protection. I could not bring myself to be of his opinion; I had not the courage to follow the advice he gave. The next day the lady returned, and my brother sold his vase to her for ten thousand pieces of gold. This money he laid out in the most advantageous manner, by purchasing a new stock of merchandise. I repented, when it was too late; but I believe it is part of the fatality attending certain persons, that they cannot decide rightly at the proper moment. When the opportunity has been lost, I have always regretted that I did not do exactly the contrary to what I had previously determined upon. Often, whilst I was hesitating, the favorable moment passed. Now this is what I call being unlucky. But to proceed with my story.

"The lady, who bought my brother Saladin's vase, was the favorite of the sultan, and all-powerful in the seraglio. Her dislike to me, in consequence of my opposition to her wishes, was so violent, that she refused to return to my brother's house while I remained there. He was unwilling to part with me; but I could not bear to be the ruin of so good a brother. Without telling him my design, I left his house, careless of what should become of me. Hunger, however, soon compelled me to think of some immediate mode of obtaining relief. I sat down upon a stone, before the door of a baker's shop; the smell of hot bread tempted me in, and with a feeble voice I demanded charity.

"The master baker gave me as much bread as I could eat, upon condition that I should change dresses with

him, and carry the rolls for him through the city this
day. To this I readily consented; but I had soon reason to repent of my compliance. Indeed, if my ill luck
had not, as usual, deprived me at this critical moment
of memory and judgment, I should never have complied
with the baker's treacherous proposal. For some time
before, the people of Constantinople had been much
dissatisfied with the weight and quality of the bread
furnished by the bakers. This species of discontent has
often been the sure forerunner of an insurrection; and,
in these disturbances, the master bakers frequently lose
their lives. All these circumstances I knew; but they
did not occur to my memory, when they might have
been useful.

"I changed dresses with the baker; but scarcely had
I proceeded through the adjoining streets with my rolls,
before the mob began to gather round me, with re-
proaches and execrations. The crowd pursued me even
to the gates of the grand seignior's palace; and the
grand vizier, alarmed at their violence, sent out an
order to have my head struck off; the usual remedy, in
such cases, being to strike off the baker's head.

"I now fell upon my knees, and protested I was not
the baker for whom they took me; that I had no connection with him; and that I had never furnished the
people of Constantinople with bread that was not weight.
I declared I had merely changed clothes with a master
baker, for this day; and that I should not have done so,
but for the evil destiny which governs all my actions.
Some of the mob exclaimed that I deserved to lose my
head for my folly; but others took pity on me, and

whilst the officer, who was sent to execute the vizier's order, turned to speak to some of the noisy rioters, those who were touched by my misfortune opened a passage for me through the crowd, and, thus favored, I effected my escape.

"I quitted Constantinople: my vase I had left in the care of my brother. At some miles' distance from the city, I overtook a party of soldiers. I joined them; and learning that they were going to embark with the rest of the grand seignior's army for Egypt, I resolved to accompany them. If it be, thought I, the will of Mahomet that I should perish, the sooner I meet my fate the better. The despondency into which I was sunk was attended by so great a degree of indolence, that I scarcely would take the necessary means to preserve my existence. During our passage to Egypt, I sat all day long upon the deck of the vessel, smoking my pipe; and I am convinced that if a storm had risen, as I expected, I should not have taken my pipe from my mouth, nor should I have handled a rope, to save myself from destruction. Such is the effect of that species of resignation or torpor, whichever you please to call it, to which my strong belief in *fatality* had reduced my mind.

"We landed, however, safely, contrary to my melancholy forebodings. By a trifling accident, not worth relating, I was detained longer than any of my companions in the vessel when we disembarked; and I did not arrive at the camp till late at night. It was moonlight, and I could see the whole scene distinctly. There was a vast number of small tents scattered over a desert of white sand; a few date-trees were visible at a distance;

all was gloomy, and all still; no sound was to be heard but that of the camels, feeding near the tents; and, as I walked on, I met with no human creature.

"My pipe was now out, and I quickened my pace a little towards a fire, which I saw near one of the tents. As I proceeded, my eye was caught by something sparkling in the sand: it was a ring. I picked it up, and put it on my finger, resolving to give it to the public crier the next morning, who might find out its rightful owner: but by ill luck, I put it on my little finger, for which it was much too large; and as I hastened towards the fire to light my pipe, I dropped the ring. I stooped to search for it amongst the provender on which a mule was feeding; and the cursed animal gave me so violent a kick on the head, that I could not help roaring aloud.

"My cries awakened those who slept in the tent, near which the mule was feeding. Provoked at being disturbed, the soldiers were ready enough to think ill of me; and they took it for granted that I was a thief, who had stolen the ring I pretended to have just found. The ring was taken from me by force; and the next day I was bastinadoed for having found it: the officer persisting in the belief that stripes would make me confess where I had concealed certain other articles of value, which had lately been missed in the camp. All this was the consequence of my being in a hurry to light my pipe, and of my having put the ring on a finger that was too little for it; which no one but Murad the Unlucky would have done.

"When I was able to walk again after my wounds were healed, I went into one of the tents distinguished by a red flag, having been told that these were coffee-houses. Whilst I was drinking coffee, I heard a stranger near me complaining that he had not been able to recover a valuable ring he had lost; although he had caused his loss to be published for three days by the public crier, offering a reward of two hundred sequins to whoever should restore it. I guessed that this was the very ring which I had unfortunately found. I addressed myself to the stranger, and promised to point out to him the person who had forced it from me. The stranger recovered his ring; and, being convinced that I had acted honestly, he made me a present of two hundred sequins, as some amends for the punishment which I had unjustly suffered on his account.

" Now you would imagine that this purse of gold was advantageous to me: far the contrary; it was the cause of new misfortunes.

" One night, when I thought that the soldiers who were in the same tent with me were all fast asleep, I indulged myself in the pleasure of counting my treasure. The next day I was invited by my companions to drink sherbet with them. What they mixed with the sherbet which I drank, I know not; but I could not resist the drowsiness it brought on. I fell into a profound slumber; and, when I awoke, I found myself lying under a date-tree, at some distance from the camp.

" The first thing I thought of, when I came to my recollection, was my purse of sequins. The purse I found still safe in my girdle; but, on opening it, I perceived that it was filled with pebbles, and not a single sequin was left. I had no doubt that I had been robbed

by the soldiers with whom I had drunk sherbet; and I
am certain that some of them must have been awake the
night I counted my money; otherwise, as I had never
trusted the secret of my riches to any one, they could
not have suspected me of possessing any property; for,
ever since I kept company with them, I had appeared to
be in great indigence.

"I applied in vain to the superior officers for redress:
the soldiers protested they were innocent; no positive
proof appeared against them, and I gained nothing by
my complaint but ridicule and ill-will. I called myself,
in the first transport of my grief, by that name which,
since my arrival in Egypt, I had avoided to pronounce:
I called myself Murad the Unlucky! The name and the
story ran through the camp; and I was accosted afterwards, very frequently, by this appellation. Some indeed
varied their wit by calling me Murad with the purse of
pebbles.

"All that I had yet suffered is nothing compared to
my succeeding misfortunes.

"It was the custom at this time, in the Turkish camp,
for the soldiers to amuse themselves with firing at a
mark. The superior officers remonstrated against this
dangerous practice, but ineffectually. Sometimes a party
of soldiers would stop firing for a few minutes, after a
message was brought them from their commanders; and
then they would begin again, in defiance of all orders.
Such was the want of discipline in our army, that this dis-
obedience went unpunished. In the mean time, the frequency of the danger made most men totally regardless
of it. I have seen tents pierced with bullets, in which

parties were quietly seated smoking their pipes, whilst those without were preparing to take fresh aim at the red flag on the top.

"This apathy proceeded, in some, from unconquerable indolence of body; in others, from the intoxication produced by the fumes of tobacco and of opium; but in most of my brother Turks it arose from the confidence which the belief in predestination inspired. When a bullet killed one of their companions, they only observed, scarcely taking the pipes from their mouths, 'Our hour is not yet come: it is not the will of Mahomet that we should fall.'

"I own that this rash security appeared to me, at first, surprising; but it soon ceased to strike me with wonder; and it even tended to confirm my favorite opinion, that some were born to good and some to evil fortune. I became almost as careless as my companions, from following the same course of reasoning. It is not, thought I, in the power of human prudence to avert the stroke of destiny. I shall perhaps die to-morrow; let me therefore enjoy to-day.

"I now made it my study, every day, to procure as much amusement as possible. My poverty, as you will imagine, restricted me from indulgence and excess; but I soon found means to spend what did not actually belong to me. There were certain Jews who were followers of the camp, and who, calculating on the probability of victory for our troops, advanced money to the soldiers; for which they engaged to pay these usurers exorbitant interest. The Jew to whom I applied traded with me also upon the belief that my brother Saladin, with whose

character and circumstances he was acquainted, would
pay my debts, if I should fall. With the money I raised
from the Jew I continually bought coffee and opium, of
which I grew immoderately fond. In the delirium it
created, I forgot all my misfortunes, all fear of the
future.

"One day, when I had raised my spirits by an unusual
quantity of opium, I was strolling through the camp,
sometimes singing, sometimes dancing, like a madman,
and repeating that I was not now Murad the Unlucky.
Whilst these words were on my lips, a friendly spectator,
who was in possession of his sober senses, caught me
by the arm, and attempted to drag me from the place
where I was exposing myself. 'Do you not see,' said
he, 'those soldiers, who are firing at a mark?   I saw one
of them, just now, deliberately taking aim at your turban; and, observe, he is now reloading his piece.' My
ill luck prevailed even at this instant, the only instant
in my life when I defied its power. I struggled with my
adviser, repeating, 'I am not the wretch you take me
for; I am not Murad the Unlucky.' He fled from the
danger himself: I remained, and in a few seconds afterwards a ball reached me, and I fell senseless on the
sand.

"The ball was cut out of my body by an awkward
surgeon, who gave me ten times more pain than was
necessary. He was particularly hurried, at this time,
because the army had just received orders to march in
a few hours, and all was confusion in the camp. My
wound was excessively painful, and the fear of being left
behind with those who were deemed incurable added to

my torments. Perhaps, if I had kept myself quiet, I
might have escaped some of the evils I afterwards en-
dured; but, as I have repeatedly told you, gentlemen,
it was my ill fortune never to be able to judge what
was best to be done, till the time for prudence was
past.

"During that day, when my fever was at the height, and
when my orders were to keep my bed, contrary to my
natural habits of indolence, I rose a hundred times, and
went out of my tent in the very heat of the day, to satisfy my curiosity as to the number of the tents which had
not been struck, and of the soldiers who had not yet
marched. The orders to march were tardily obeyed, and
many hours elapsed before our encampment was raised.
Had I submitted to my surgeon's orders, I might have
been in a state to accompany the most dilatory of the
stragglers; I could have borne, perhaps, the slow motion
of a litter, on which some of the sick were transported;
but in the evening, when the surgeon came to dress my
wounds, he found me in such a situation that it was
scarcely possible to remove me.

"He desired a party of soldiers, who were left to
bring up the rear, to call for me the next morning.
They did so; but they wanted to put me upon the mule
which I recollected, by a white streak on its back, to be
the cursed animal that had kicked me whilst I was looking for the ring. I could not be prevailed upon to go
upon this unlucky animal. I tried to persuade the soldiers to carry me, and they took me a little way; but,
soon growing weary of their burden, they laid me down
on the sand, pretending that they were going to fill a

skin with water at a spring they had discovered, and bade me lie still, and wait for their return.

"I waited and waited, longing for the water to moisten my parched lips; but no water came, — no soldiers returned; and there I lay, for several hours, expecting every moment to breathe my last. I made no effort to move, for I was now convinced my hour was come, and that it was the will of Mahomet that I should perish in this miserable manner, and lie unburied like a dog; a death, thought I, worthy of Murad the Unlucky.

"My forebodings were not this time just; a detachment of English soldiers passed near the place where I lay: my groans were heard by them, and they humanely came to my assistance. They carried me with them, dressed my wound, and treated me with the utmost tenderness. Christians though they were, I must acknowledge that I had reason to love them better than any of the followers of Mahomet, my good brother only excepted.

"Under their care I recovered; but scarcely had I regained my strength before I fell into new disasters. It was hot weather, and my thirst was excessive. I went out with a party, in hopes of finding a spring of water. The English soldiers began to dig for a well, in a place pointed out to them by one of their men of science. I was not inclined to such hard labor, but preferred sauntering on in search of a spring. I saw at a distance something that looked like a pool of water; and I pointed it out to my companions. Their man of science warned me by his interpreter not to trust to this deceitful appearance; for that such were common in this country, and that, when I came close to the spot, I should find no water there.   He added that it was at a greater distance than I imagined; and that I should, in all probability, be lost in the desert, if I attempted to follow this phantom.

"I was so unfortunate as not to attend to his advice: I set out in pursuit of this accursed delusion, which assuredly was the work of evil spirits, who clouded my reason, and allured me into their dominion.   I went on, hour after hour, in expectation continually of reaching the object of my wishes; but it fled faster than I pursued, and I discovered at last that the Englishman, who had doubtless gained his information from the people of the country, was right; and that the shining appearance, which I had taken for water, was a mere deception.

"I was now exhausted with fatigue: I looked back in vain after the companions I had left; I could see neither men, animals, nor any trace of vegetation in the sandy desert.   I had no resource but, weary as I was, to measure back my footsteps, which were imprinted in the sand.

"I slowly and sorrowfully traced them as my guides in this unknown land.   Instead of yielding to my indolent inclinations, I ought, however, to have made the best of my way back, before the evening breeze sprung up.   I felt the breeze rising, and, unconscious of my danger, I rejoiced, and opened my bosom to meet it; but what was my dismay when I saw that the wind swept before it all trace of my footsteps in the sand.   I knew not which way to proceed; I was struck with despair, tore my garments, threw off my turban, and cried aloud; but neither human voice nor echo answered me.   The silence was dreadful.   I had tasted no food for many hours, and I now became sick and faint.   I recollected that I had put a supply of opium into the folds of my turban; but, alas! when I took my turban up, I found that the opium had fallen out. I searched for it in vain on the sand, where I had thrown the turban.

"I stretched myself out upon the ground, and yielded without further struggle to my evil destiny. What I suffered from thirst, hunger, and heat cannot be described! At last I fell into a sort of trance, during which images of various kinds seemed to flit before my eyes. How long I remained in this state I know not; but I remember that I was brought to my senses by a loud shout, which came from persons belonging to a caravan returning from Mecca. This was a shout of joy for their safe arrival at a certain spring, well known to them in this part of the desert.

"The spring was not a hundred yards from the spot where I lay; yet, such had been the fate of Murad the Unlucky, that he missed the reality, whilst he had been hours in pursuit of the phantom. Feeble and spiritless as I was, I sent forth as loud a cry as I could, in hopes of obtaining assistance; and I endeavored to crawl to the place from which the voices appeared to come. The caravan rested for a considerable time whilst the slaves filled the skins with water, and whilst the camels took in their supply. I worked myself on towards them; yet, notwithstanding my efforts, I was persuaded that, according to my usual ill fortune, I should never be able to make them hear my voice. I saw them mount their camels! I took off my turban, unrolled it, and waved it in the air. My signal was seen! The caravan came towards me!

"I had scarcely strength to speak: a slave gave me some water; and, after I had drunk, I explained to them who I was, and how I·came into this situation.

"Whilst I was speaking, one of the travellers observed the purse which hung to my girdle: it was the same the merchant, for whom I recovered the ring, had given to me; I had carefully preserved it, because the initials of my benefactor's name, and a passage from the Koran, were worked upon it. When he gave it to me, he said that perhaps we should meet again in some other part of the world, and he should recognize me by this token. The person who now took notice of the purse was his brother; and when I related to him how I had obtained it, he had the goodness to take me under his protection. He was a merchant, who was now going with the caravan to Grand Cairo: he offered to take me with him, and I willingly accepted the proposal, promising to serve him as faithfully as any of his slaves. The caravan proceeded, and I was carried with it.

II.

"THE merchant, who was become my master, treated me with great kindness; but, on hearing me relate the whole series of my unfortunate adventures, he exacted a promise from me, that I would do nothing without first consulting him. 'Since you are so unlucky, Murad,' said he, 'that you always choose for the worst when you choose for yourself, you should trust entirely to the judgment of a wiser or a more fortunate friend.'

"I fared well in the service of this merchant, who

5 *

was a man of a mild disposition, and who was so rich
that he could afford to be generous to all his dependants.
It was my business to see his camels loaded and un-
loaded at proper places, to count his bales of merchandise, and to take care that they were not mixed with
those of his companions. This I carefully did, till the
day we arrived at Alexandria; when, unluckily, I neglected to count the bales, taking it for granted that they
were all right, as I had found them so the preceding
day. However, when we were to go on board the vessel that was to take us to Cairo, I perceived that three
bales of cotton were missing.

"I ran to inform my master, who, though a good deal
provoked at my negligence, did not reproach me as I
deserved. The public crier was immediately sent round
the city, to offer a reward for the recovery of the merchandise; and it was restored by one of the merchants'
slaves, with whom we had travelled. The vessel was
now under sail; my master and I and the bales of cotton were obliged to follow in a boat; and when we were
taken on board, the captain declared he was so loaded
that he could not tell where to stow the bales of cotton.
After much difficulty, he consented to let them remain
upon deck: and I promised my master to watch them
night and day.

"We had a prosperous voyage, and were actually in
sight of shore, which the captain said we could not fail
to reach early the next morning. I stayed, as usual,
this night upon deck; and solaced myself by smoking
my pipe. Ever since I had indulged in this practice at
the camp at El Arish, I could not exist without opium

and tobacco. I suppose that my reason was this night a little clouded with the dose I took; but, towards midnight, I was sobered by terror. I started up from the deck on which I had stretched myself; my turban was in flames; the bale of cotton on which I had rested was all on fire. I awakened two sailors, who were fast asleep on deck. The consternation became general, and the confusion increased the danger. The captain and my master were the most active, and suffered the most in extinguishing the flames: my master was terribly scorched.

"For my part, I was not suffered to do anything; the captain ordered that I should be bound to the mast; and, when at last the flames were extinguished, the passengers, with one accord, besought him to keep me bound hand and foot, lest I should be the cause of some new disaster. All that had happened was, indeed, occasioned by my ill luck. I had laid my pipe down, when I was falling asleep, upon the bale of cotton that was beside me. The fire from my pipe fell out, and set the cotton in flames. Such was the mixture of rage and terror with which I had inspired the whole crew, that I am sure they would have set me ashore on a desert island, rather than have had me on board for a week longer. Even my humane master, I could perceive, was secretly impatient to get rid of Murad the Unlucky, and his evil fortune.

"You may believe that I was heartily glad when we landed, and when I was unbound. My master put a purse containing fifty sequins into my hand, and bade me farewell. 'Use this money prudently, Murad, if you can,' said he, 'and perhaps your fortune may change.'

Of this I had little hopes, but determined to lay out my money as prudently as possible.

"As I was walking through the streets of Grand Cairo, considering how I should lay out my fifty sequins to the greatest advantage, I was stopped by one who called me by my name, and asked me if I could pretend to have forgotten his face. I looked steadily at him, and recollected to my sorrow that he was the Jew Rachub, from whom I had borrowed certain sums of money at the camp at El Arish. What brought him to Grand Cairo, except it was my evil destiny, I cannot tell. He would not quit me; he would take no excuses; he said he knew that I had deserted twice, once from the Turkish and once from the English army; that I was not entitled to any pay; and that he could not imagine it possible that my brother Saladin would own me, or pay my debts.

"I replied, for I was vexed by the insolence of this Jewish dog, that I was not, as he imagined, a beggar; that I had the means of paying him my just debt, but that I hoped he would not extort from me all that exorbitant interest which none but a Jew could exact. He smiled, and answered that, if a Turk loved opium better than money, this was no fault of his; that he had supplied me with what I loved best in the world; and that I ought not to complain, when he expected I should return the favor.

"I will not weary you, gentlemen, with all the arguments that passed between me and Rachub. At last we compromised matters; he would take nothing less than the whole debt: but he let me have at a very cheap rate a chest of second-hand clothes, by which he assured me I might make my fortune. He brought them to Grand Cairo, he said, for the purpose of selling them to slave-merchants, who at this time of the year were in want of them to supply their slaves; but he was in haste to get home to his wife and family, at Constantinople, and therefore he was willing to make over to a friend the profits of this speculation. I should have distrusted Rachub's professions of friendship and especially of dis-interestedness; but he took me with him to the khan, where his goods were, and unlocked the chest of clothes to show them to me. They were of the richest and fin-est materials, and had been but little worn. I could not doubt the evidence of my senses; the bargain was con-cluded, and the Jew sent porters to my inn with the chest.

"The next day I repaired to the public market-place; and, when my business was known, I had choice of cus-tomers before night: my chest was empty, — and my purse was full. The profit I made, upon the sale of these clothes, was so considerable, that I could not help feeling astonishment at Rachub's having brought himself so readily to relinquish them.

"A few days after I had disposed of the contents of my chest, a Damascene merchant, who had bought two suits of apparel from me, told me, with a very melan-choly face, that both the female slaves who had put on these clothes were sick. I could not conceive that the clothes were the cause of their sickness; but soon after-wards, as I was crossing the market, I was attacked by at least a dozen merchants, who made similar complaints.

They insisted upon knowing how I came by the garments, and demanded whether I had worn any of them myself. This day I had for the first time indulged myself with wearing a pair of yellow slippers, the only finery I had reserved for myself out of all the tempting goods. Convinced by my wearing these slippers that I could have had no insidious designs, since I shared the danger, whatever it might be, the merchants were a little pacified; but what was my terror and remorse the next day, when one of them came to inform me that plague-boils had broken out under the arms of all the slaves who had worn this pestilential apparel! On looking carefully into the chest, we found the word Smyrna written, and half effaced, upon the lid. Now, the plague had for some time raged at Smyrna; and, as the merchants suspected, these clothes had certainly belonged to persons who had died of that distemper. This was the reason why the Jew was willing to sell them to me so cheap; and it was for this reason that he would not stay at Grand Cairo himself to reap *the profits of his speculation*. Indeed, if I had paid attention to it at the proper time, a slight circumstance might have revealed the truth to me. Whilst I was bargaining with the Jew, before he opened the chest, he swallowed a large dram of brandy, and stuffed his nostrils with sponge dipped in vinegar : this he told me he did to prevent his perceiving the smell of musk, which always threw him into convulsions.

"The horror I felt, when I discovered that I had spread the infection of the plague, and that I had probably caught it myself, overpowered my senses; a cold dew spread over all my limbs, and I fell upon the lid of the fatal chest in a swoon. It is said that fear disposes people to take the infection; however this may be, I sickened that evening, and soon was in a raging fever. It was worse for me whenever the delirium left me, and I could reflect upon the miseries my ill fortune had occasioned. In my first lucid interval, I looked round and saw that I had been removed from the khan to a wretched hut. An old woman, who was smoking her pipe in the farthest corner of my room, informed me that I had been sent out of the town of Grand Cairo by order of the cadi, to whom the merchants had made their complaint. The fatal chest was burnt, and the house in which I had lodged razed to the ground. 'And if it had not been for me,' continued the old woman, 'you would have been dead, probably, at this instant; but I have made a vow to our great prophet, that I would never neglect an opportunity of doing a good action: therefore, when you were deserted by all the world, I took care of you. Here, too, is your purse, which I saved from the rabble; and, what is more difficult, from the officers of justice: I will account to you for every para that I have expended; and will moreover tell you the reason of my making such an extraordinary vow.'

"As I believed that this benevolent old woman took great pleasure in talking, I made an inclination of my head to thank her for her promised history, and she proceeded; but I must confess I did not listen with all the attention her narrative doubtless deserved. Even curiosity, the strongest passion of us Turks, was dead within me. I have no recollection of the old woman's story. It is as much as I can do to finish my own.

"The weather became excessively hot; it was affirmed, by some of the physicians, that this heat would prove fatal to their patients; but, contrary to the prognostics of the physicians, it stopped the progress of the plague. I recovered, and found my purse much lightened by my illness. I divided the remainder of my money with my humane nurse, and sent her out into the city, to inquire how matters were going on.

"She brought me word that the fury of the plague had much abated; but that she had met several funerals, and that she had heard many of the merchants cursing the folly of Murad the Unlucky, who, as they said, had brought all this calamity upon the inhabitants of Cairo. Even fools, they say, learn my experience. I took care to burn the bed on which I had lain, and the clothes I had worn: I concealed my real name, which I knew would inspire detestation, and gained admittance, with a crowd of other poor wretches, into a lazaretto, where I performed quarantine, and offered up prayers daily for the sick.

"When I thought it was impossible I could spread the infection, I took my passage home. I was eager to get away from Grand Cairo, where I knew I was an object of execration. I had a strange fancy haunting my mind; I imagined that all my misfortunes, since I left Constantinople, had arisen from my neglect of the talisman upon the beautiful china vase. I dreamed three times, when I was recovering from the plague, that a genius appeared to me, and said, in a reproachful tone,

'Murad, where is the vase that was intrusted to thy care?'

"This dream operated strongly upon my imagination. As soon as we arrived at Constantinople, which we did, to my great surprise, without meeting with any untoward accidents, I went in search of my brother Saladin, to inquire for my vase. He no longer lived in the house in which I left him, and I began to be apprehensive that he was dead; but a porter, hearing my inquiries, exclaimed, 'Who is there in Constantinople that is ignorant of the dwelling of Saladin the Lucky? Come with me, and I will show it to you.'

"The mansion to which he conducted me looked so magnificent, that I was almost afraid to enter lest there should be some mistake. But, whilst I was hesitating, the doors opened, and I heard my brother Saladin's voice. He saw me almost at the same instant that I fixed my eyes upon him, and immediately sprang forward to embrace me. He was the same good brother as ever, and I rejoiced in his prosperity with all my heart. 'Brother Saladin,' said I, 'can you now doubt that some men are born to be fortunate, and others to be unfortunate? How often you used to dispute this point with me!'

"'Let us not dispute it now in the public street,' said he, smiling; 'but come in and refresh yourself, and we will consider the question afterwards at leisure.'

"'No, my dear brother,' said I, drawing back, 'you are too good: Murad the Unlucky shall not enter your house, lest he should draw down misfortunes upon you and yours. I come only to ask for my vase.'

H

" 'It is safe,' cried he; 'come in, and you shall see it; but I will not give it up till I have you in my house. I have none of these superstitious fears: pardon me the expression, but I have none of these superstitious fears.'

" I yielded, entered his house, and was astonished at all I saw! My brother did not triumph in his prosperity; but, on the contrary, seemed intent only upon making me forget my misfortunes: he listened to the account of them with kindness, and obliged me by the recital of his history; which was, I must acknowledge, far less wonderful than my own. He seemed, by his own account, to have grown rich in the common course of things; or, rather, by his own prudence. I allowed for his prejudices, and, unwilling to dispute further with him, said, ' You must remain of your opinion, brother; and I of mine: you are Saladin the Lucky, and I Murad the Unlucky; and so we shall remain to the end of our lives.'

" I had not been in his house four days when an accident happened, which showed how much I was in the right. The favorite of the sultan, to whom he had formerly sold his china vase, though her charms were now somewhat faded by time, still retained her power, and her taste for magnificence. She commissioned my brother to bespeak for her, at Venice, the most splendid looking-glass that money could purchase. The mirror, after many delays and disappointments, at length arrived at my brother's house. He unpacked it, and sent to let the lady know it was in perfect safety. It was late in the evening, and she ordered it should remain where it was that night; and that it should be brought to the

seraglio the next morning. It stood in a sort of antechamber to the room in which I slept; and with it were
left some packages, containing glass chandeliers for an
unfinished saloon in my brother's house. Saladin charged
all his domestics to be vigilant this night, because he had
money to a great amount by him, and there had been
frequent robberies in our neighborhood. Hearing these
orders, I resolved to be in readiness at a moment's warning. I laid my scimitar beside me upon a cushion; and
left my door half open, that I might hear the slightest
noise in the antechamber or the great staircase. About
midnight I was suddenly awakened by a noise in the
antechamber. I started up, seized my scimitar, and the
instant I got to the door, saw, by the light of the lamp
which was burning in the room, a man standing opposite
to me, with a drawn sword in his hand. I rushed
forward, demanding what he wanted, and received no
answer; but, seeing him aim at me with his scimitar, I
gave him, as I thought, a deadly blow. At this instant,
I heard a great crash; and the fragments of the looking-
glass, which I had shivered, fell at my feet. At the
same moment something black brushed by my shoulder:
I pursued it, stumbled over the packages of glass, and
rolled over them down the stairs.

"My brother came out of his room, to inquire the
cause of all this disturbance; and when he saw the fine
mirror broken, and me lying amongst the glass chandeliers at the bottom of the stairs, he could not forbear
exclaiming, 'Well, brother! you are indeed Murad the
Unlucky.'

"When the first emotion was over, he could not,

however, forbear laughing at my situation. With a
degree of goodness, which made me a thousand times
more sorry for the accident, he came down stairs to help
me up, gave me his hand, and said, 'Forgive me, if I
was angry with you at first. I am sure you did not
mean to do me any injury; but tell me how all this has
happened.'

"Whilst Saladin was speaking, I heard the same kind
of noise which had alarmed me in the antechamber; but,
on looking back, I saw only a black pigeon, which flew
swiftly by me, unconscious of the mischief he had occasioned. This pigeon I had unluckily brought into the
house the preceding day; and had been feeding and
trying to tame it for my young nephews. I little thought
it would be the cause of such disasters. My brother,
though he endeavored to conceal his anxiety from me,
was much disturbed at the idea of meeting the favorite's
displeasure, who would certainly be grievously disappointed by the loss of her splendid looking-glass. I saw
that I should inevitably be his ruin, if I continued in his
house; and no persuasions could prevail upon me to
prolong my stay. My generous brother, seeing me
determined to go, said to me, 'A factor, whom I have
employed for some years to sell merchandise for me, died
a few days ago. Will you take his place? I am rich
enough to bear any little mistakes you may fall into, from
ignorance of business; and you will have a partner who
is able and willing to assist you.'

"I was touched to the heart by this kindness, especially at such a time as this. He sent one of his slaves
with me to the shop in which you now see me, gentle-

men. The slave, by my brother's directions, brought
with us my china vase, and delivered it safely to me,
with this message: 'The scarlet dye that was found in
this vase, and in its fellow, was the first cause of Saladin's
making the fortune he now enjoys: he therefore does no
more than justice, in sharing that fortune with his brother
Murad.'

"I was now placed in as advantageous a situation as
possible ; but my mind was ill at ease, when I reflected
that the broken mirror might be my brother's ruin.
The lady by whom it had been bespoken was, I well
knew, of a violent temper; and this disappointment
was sufficient to provoke her to vengeance. My brother
sent me word this morning, however, that, though her
displeasure was excessive, it was in my power to prevent any ill consequences that might ensue. 'In my
power!' I exclaimed; 'then, indeed, I am happy! Tell
my brother there is nothing I will not do to show him
my gratitude, and to save him from the consequences of
my folly.'

"The slave who was sent by my brother seemed unwilling to name what was required of me, saying that his
master was afraid I should not like to grant the request.
I urged him to speak freely, and he then told me the
favorite declared nothing would make her amends for
the loss of the mirror but the fellow vase to that which
she had bought from Saladin. It was impossible for me
to hesitate ; gratitude for my brother's generous kindness overcame my superstitious obstinacy ; and I sent
him word I would carry the vase to him myself.

"I took it down this evening from the shelf on which

it stood ; it was covered with dust, and I washed it, but
unluckily, in endeavoring to clean the inside from the
remains of the scarlet powder, I poured hot water into
it, and immediately I heard a simmering noise, and my
vase, in a few instants, burst asunder with a loud explosion. These fragments, alas! are all that remain. The
measure of my misfortunes is now completed! Can you
wonder, gentlemen, that I bewail my evil destiny? Am
I not justly called Murad the Unlucky? Here end all
my hopes in this world! Better would it have been if
I had died long ago! Better that I had never been
born! Nothing I ever have done or attempted has
prospered. Murad the Unlucky is my name, and ill
fate has marked me for her own."

III.

THE lamentations of Murad were interrupted by the
entrance of Saladin. Having waited in vain for some
hours, he now came to see if any disaster had happened
to his brother Murad. He was surprised at the sight
of the two pretended merchants, and could not refrain
from exclamations on beholding the broken vase. However, with his usual equanimity and good-nature, he
began to console Murad; and, taking up the fragments,
examined them carefully, one by one joined them together again, found that none of the edges of the china
were damaged, and declared he could have it mended so
as to look as well as ever.

Murad recovered his spirits upon this. "Brother,"
said he, "I comfort myself for being Murad the Un-

lucky, when I reflect that you are Saladin the Lucky.
See, gentlemen," continued he, turning to the pretended
merchants, "scarcely has this most fortunate of men
been five minutes in company before he gives a happy
turn to affairs. His presence inspires joy : I observe
your countenances, which had been saddened by my
dismal history, have brightened up since he has made
his appearance. Brother, I wish you would make these
gentlemen some amends for the time they have wasted
in listening to my catalogue of misfortunes, by relating
your history, which, I am sure, they will find rather
more exhilarating."

Saladin consented, on condition that the strangers
would accompany him home, and partake of a social
banquet. They at first repeated the former excuse of
their being obliged to return to their inn; but at length
the sultan's curiosity prevailed, and he and his vizier
went home with Saladin the Lucky, who, after supper,
related his history in the following manner : —

" My being called Saladin the Lucky first inspired me
with confidence in myself ; though I own that I cannot
remember any extraordinary instances of good luck in
my childhood. An old nurse of my mother's, indeed,
repeated to me, twenty times a day, that nothing I undertook could fail to succeed, because I was Saladin the
Lucky. I became presumptuous and rash ; and my
nurse's prognostics might have effectually prevented
their accomplishment, had I not, when I was about
fifteen, been roused to reflection during a long confinement, which was the consequence of my youthful
conceit and imprudence.

"At this time there was at the Porte a Frenchman, an ingenious engineer, who was employed and favored by the sultan, to the great astonishment of many of my prejudiced countrymen. On the grand seignior's birthday he exhibited some extraordinarily fine fireworks; and I, with numbers of the inhabitants of Constantinople, crowded to see them. I happened to stand near the place where the Frenchman was stationed; the crowd pressed upon him, and I amongst the rest; he begged we would, for our own sakes, keep at a greater distance, and warned us that we might be much hurt by the combustibles which he was using. I, relying upon my good fortune, disregarded all these cautions; and the consequence was, that as I touched some of the materials prepared for the fireworks, they exploded, dashed me upon the ground with great violence, and I was terribly burnt.

"This accident, gentlemen, I consider as one of the most fortunate circumstances of my life; for it checked and corrected the presumption of my temper. During the time I was confined to my bed, the French gentleman came frequently to see me. He was a very sensible man; and the conversations he had with me enlarged my mind, and cured me of many foolish prejudices, especially of that which I had been taught to entertain, concerning the predominance of what is called luck, or fortune, in human affairs. 'Though you are called Saladin the Lucky,' said he, 'you find that your neglect of prudence has nearly brought you to the grave even in the bloom of youth. Take my advice, and henceforward trust more to prudence than to fortune. Let the multitude,

if they will, call you Saladin the Lucky; but call yourself, and make yourself, Saladin the Prudent.'

"These words left an indelible impression on my mind,
and gave a new turn to my thoughts and character. My
brother, Murad, has doubtless told you that our difference of opinion, on the subject of predestination, produced between us frequent arguments; but we could
never convince one another, and we each have acted,
through life, in consequence of our different beliefs.
To this I attribute my success and his misfortunes.

"The first rise of my fortune, as you have probably
heard from Murad, was owing to the scarlet dye, which
I brought to perfection with infinite difficulty. The
powder, it is true, was accidentally found by me in our
china vases; but there it might have remained to this
instant, useless, if I had not taken the pains to make it
useful. I grant that we can only partially foresee and
command events; yet on the use we make of our own
powers, I think, depends our destiny. But, gentlemen,
you would rather hear my adventures, perhaps, than my
reflections; and I am truly concerned, for your sakes,
that I have no wonderful events to relate. I am sorry
I cannot tell you of my having been lost in a sandy
desert. I have never had the plague, nor even been
shipwrecked: I have been all my life an inhabitant of
Constantinople, and have passed my time in a very
quiet and uniform manner.

"The money I received from the sultan's favorite for
my china vase, as my brother may have told you, enabled
me to trade on a more extensive scale. I went on
steadily with my business; and made it my whole study

to please my employers, by all fair and honorable means. This industry and civility succeeded beyond my expectations : in a few years, I was rich for a man in my way of business.

"I will not proceed to trouble you with the journal of a petty merchant's life; I pass on to the incident which made a considerable change in my affairs.

"A terrible fire broke out near the walls of the grand seignior's seraglio : as you are strangers, gentlemen, you may not have heard of this event, though it produced so great a sensation in Constantinople. The vizier's superb palace was utterly consumed; and the melted lead poured down from the roof of the mosque of St. Sophia. Various were the opinions formed by my neighbors respecting the cause of the conflagration. Some supposed it to be a punishment for the sultan's having neglected, one Friday, to appear at the mosque of St. Sophia; others considered it as a warning sent by Mahomet, to dissuade the Porte from persisting in a war in which we were just engaged. The generality, however, of the coffee-house politicians contented themselves with observing that it was the will of Mahomet that the palace should be consumed. Satisfied by this supposition, they took no precaution to prevent similar accidents in their own houses. Never were fires so common in the city as at this period; scarcely a night passed without our being wakened by the cry of fire.

"These frequent fires were rendered still more dreadful by villains, who were continually on the watch to increase the confusion by which they profited, and to pillage the houses of the sufferers. It was discovered

that these incendiaries frequently skulked, towards evening, in the neighborhood of the bezestein, where the
richest merchants store their goods; some of these
wretches were detected in throwing *coundaks*, or matches,
into the windows; and if these combustibles remained a
sufficient time, they could not fail to set the house on
fire.

"Notwithstanding all these circumstances, many even
of those who had property to preserve continued to repeat, 'It is the will of Mahomet,' and consequently to
neglect all means of preservation. I, on the contrary,
recollecting the lesson I had learned from the sensible
foreigner, neither suffered my spirits to sink with superstitious fears of ill luck, nor did I trust presumptuously
to my good fortune. I took every possible means to secure myself. I never went to bed without having seen
that all the lights and fires in the house were extinguished, and that I had a supply of water in the cistern.
I had likewise learned from my Frenchman that wet
mortar was the most effectual thing for stopping the
progress of flames : I therefore had a quantity of mortar
made up in one of my outhouses, which I could use at
a moment's warning. These precautions were all useful
to me : my own house, indeed, was never actually on
fire, but the houses of my next-door neighbors were no
less than five times in flames, in the course of one winter. By my exertions, or rather by my precautions, they
suffered but little damage ; and all my neighbors looked
upon me as their deliverer and friend : they loaded me
with presents, and offered more, indeed, than I would
accept. All repeated that I was Saladin the Lucky.

This compliment I disclaimed, feeling more ambitious of being called Saladin the Prudent. It is thus that what we call modesty is often only a more refined species of pride. But to proceed with my story.

"One night I had been later than usual at supper, at a friend's house: none but the watch were in the streets, and even they, I believe, were asleep.

"As I passed one of the conduits, which convey water to the city, I heard a trickling noise; and, upon examination, I found that the cock of the water-spout was half turned, so that the water was running out. I turned it back to its proper place, thought it had been left unturned by accident, and walked on; but I had not proceeded far before I came to another spout and another, which were in the same condition. I was convinced that this could not be the effect merely of accident, and suspected that some ill-intentioned persons designed to let out and waste the water of the city, that there might be none to extinguish any fire that should break out in the course of the night.

"I stood still for a few moments, to consider how it would be most prudent to act. It would be impossible for me to run to all parts of the city, that I might stop the pipes that were running to waste. I first thought of wakening the watch and the firemen, who were most of them slumbering at their stations; but I reflected that they were perhaps not to be trusted, and that they were in a confederacy with the incendiaries; otherwise, they would certainly, before this hour, have observed and stopped the running of the sewers in their neighborhood. I determined to waken a rich merchant, called Damat

Zade, who lived near me, and who had a number of slaves whom he could send to different parts of the city, to prevent mischief, and give notice to the inhabitants of their danger.

"He was a very sensible, active man, and one that could easily be wakened: he was not, like some Turks, an hour in recovering their lethargic senses. He was quick in decision and action; and his slaves resembled their master. He despatched a messenger immediately to the grand vizier, that the sultan's safety might be secured; and sent others to the magistrates, in each quarter of Constantinople. The large drums in the janissary aga's tower beat to rouse the inhabitants; and scarcely had this been heard to beat half an hour before the fire broke out in the lower apartments of Damat Zade's house, owing to a *coundak*, which had been left behind one of the doors.

"The wretches who had prepared the mischief came to enjoy it, and to pillage; but they were disappointed. Astonished to find themselves taken into custody, they could not comprehend how their designs had been frustrated. By timely exertions, the fire in my friend's house was extinguished; and though fires broke out, during the night, in many parts of the city, but little damage was sustained, because there was time for precautions; and by the stopping of the spouts, sufficient water was preserved. People were awakened, and warned of the danger, and they consequently escaped unhurt.

"The next day, as soon as I made my appearance at the bezestein, the merchants crowded round, called me their benefactor, and the preserver of their lives and fortunes. Damat Zade, the merchant whom I had awakened the preceding night, presented to me a heavy purse of gold, and put upon my finger a diamond ring of considerable value; each of the merchants followed his example, in making me rich presents: the magistrates also sent me tokens of their approbation; and the grand vizier sent me a diamond of the first water, with a line written by his own hand: 'To the man who has saved Constantinople.' Excuse me, gentlemen, for the vanity I seem to show in mentioning these circumstances. You desired to hear my history, and I cannot therefore omit the principal circumstance of my life. In the course of four-and-twenty hours, I found myself raised, by the munificent gratitude of the inhabitants of this city, to a state of affluence far beyond what I had ever dreamed of attaining.

"I now took a house suited to my circumstances, and bought a few slaves. As I was carrying my slaves home, I was met by a Jew, who stopped me, saying, in his language, 'My lord, I see, has been purchasing slaves: I could clothe them cheaply.' There was something mysterious in the manner of this Jew, and I did not like his countenance; but I considered that I ought not to be governed by caprice in my dealings, and that, if this man could really clothe my slaves more cheaply than another, I ought not to neglect his offer merely because I took a dislike to the cut of his beard, the turn of his eye, or the tone of his voice. I therefore bade the Jew follow me home, saying that I would consider of his proposal.

"When we came to talk over the matter, I was surprised to find him so reasonable in his demands. On one point, indeed, he appeared unwilling to comply. I required not only to see the clothes I was offered, but also to know how they came into his possession. On this subject he equivocated; I therefore suspected there must be something wrong. I reflected what it could be, and judged that the goods had been stolen, or that they had been the apparel of persons who had died of some contagious distemper. The Jew showed me a chest, from which he said I might choose whatever suited me best. I observed, that, as he was going to unlock the chest, he stuffed his nose with some aromatic herbs. He told me that he did so to prevent his smelling the musk with which the chest was perfumed: musk, he said, had an extraordinary effect upon his nerves. I begged to have some of the herbs which he used himself; declaring that musk was likewise offensive to me.

" The Jew, either struck by his own conscience, or observing my suspicions, turned as pale as death. He pretended he had not the right key, and could not unlock the chest; said he must go in search of it, and that he would call on me again.

" After he had left me, I examined some writing upon the lid of the chest, that had been nearly effaced. I made out the word Smyrna, and this was sufficient to confirm all my suspicions. The Jew returned no more : he sent some porters to carry away the chest, and I heard nothing of him for some time, till one day, when I was at the house of Damat Zade, I saw a glimpse of the Jew passing hastily through one of the courts, as if he wished to avoid me. ' My friend,' said I to Damat Zade, ' do not attribute my question to impertinent curiosity, or to a desire to intermeddle with your affairs, if I venture to ask the nature of your business with the Jew, who has just now crossed your court.'

"'He has engaged to supply me with clothing for my slaves,' replied my friend, 'cheaper than I can purchase it elsewhere. I have a design to surprise my daughter, Fatima, on her birthday, with an entertainment in the pavilion in the garden; and all her female slaves shall appear in new dresses on the occasion.'

"I interrupted my friend, to tell him what I suspected relative to this Jew and his chest of clothes. It is certain that the infection of the plague can be communicated by clothes, not only after months but after years have elapsed. The merchant resolved to have nothing more to do with this wretch, who could thus hazard the lives of thousands of his fellow-creatures for a few pieces of gold: we sent notice of the circumstance to the cadi, but the cadi was slow in his operations; and, before he could take the Jew into custody, the cunning fellow had effected his escape. When his house was searched, he and his chest had disappeared: we discovered that he sailed for Egypt, and rejoiced that we had driven him from Constantinople.

"My friend, Damat Zade, expressed the warmest gratitude to me. 'You formerly saved my fortune: you have now saved my life; and a life yet dearer than my own, that of my daughter Fatima.'

"At the sound of that name I could not, I believe, avoid showing some emotion. I had accidentally seen this lady, and I had been captivated by her beauty, and

by the sweetness of her countenance; but as I knew she
was destined to be the wife of another, I suppressed my
feeling, and determined to banish the recollection of the
fair Fatima forever from my imagination. Her father,
however, at this instant, threw into my way a temptation
which it required all my fortitude to resist. ' Saladin,'
continued he, ' it is but just that you, who have saved
our lives, should share our festivity. Come here on the
birthday of my Fatima: I will place you in a balcony,
which overlooks the garden, and you shall see the whole
spectacle. We shall have a *feast of tulips*, in imitation
of that which, as you know, is held in the grand seignior's gardens. I assure you, the sight will be worth
seeing; and besides, you will have a chance of beholding
my Fatima, for a moment, without her veil.'

" ' That,' interrupted I, ' is the thing I most wish to
avoid. I dare not indulge myself in a pleasure which
might cost me the happiness of my life. I will conceal
nothing from you, who treat me with so much confidence. I have already beheld the charming countenance
of your Fatima, but I know that she is destined to be
the wife of a happier man.'

" Damat Zade seemed much pleased by the frankness
with which I explained myself; but he would not give
up the idea of my sitting with him, in the balcony, on
the day of the feast of tulips, and I, on my part, could
not consent to expose myself to another view of the
charming Fatima. My friend used every argument, or
rather every sort of persuasion, he could imagine to
prevail upon me: he then tried to laugh me out of my
resolution; and, when all failed, he said, in a voice of

anger, ' Go, then, Saladin; I am sure you are deceiving me : you have a passion for some other woman, and you would conceal it from me, and persuade me you refuse the favor I offer you from prudence, when, in fact, it is from indifference and contempt. Why could you not speak the truth of your heart to me with that frankness with which one friend should treat another?'

"Astonished at this unexpected charge, and at the anger which flashed from the eyes of Damat Zade, who till this moment had always appeared to me a man of a mild and reasonable temper, I was for an instant tempted to fly into a passion and leave him : but friends, once lost, are not easily regained. This consideration had power sufficient to make me command my temper. 'My friend,' replied I, ' we will talk over this affair to-morrow : you are now angry, and cannot do me justice ; but to-morrow you will be cool : you will then be convinced that I have not deceived you ; and that I have no design but to secure my own happiness by the most prudent means in my power, by avoiding the sight of the danger-ous Fatima. I have no passion for any other woman.'

" ' Then,' said my friend, embracing me, and quitting the tone of anger which he had assumed only to try my resolution to the utmost, — ' then, Saladin, Fatima is yours.'

" I scarcely dared to believe my senses ! I could not express my joy ! ' Yes, my friend,' continued the mer-chant, 'I have tried your prudence to the utmost ; it has been victorious, and I resign my Fatima to you, certain that you will make her happy. It is true, I had a greater alliance in view for her : the pacha of Maksoud has demanded her from me; but I have found, upon private inquiry, he is addicted to the intemperate use of opium : and my daughter shall never be the wife of one who is a violent madman one half the day, and a melancholy idiot during the remainder. I have nothing to apprehend from the pacha's resentment, because I have powerful friends with the grand vizier who will oblige him to listen to reason, and to submit quietly to a disappointment he so justly merits. And now, Saladin, have you any objection to seeing the feast of tulips? '

" I replied only by falling at the merchant's feet, and embracing his knees. The feast of tulips came, and on that day I was married to the charming Fatima! The charming Fatima I continue still to think her, though she has now been my wife some years. She is the joy and pride of my heart; and, from our mutual affection, I have experienced more felicity than from all the other circumstances of my life, which are called so fortunate. Her father gave me the house in which I now live, and joined his possessions to ours; so that I have more wealth even than I desire. My riches, however, give me continually the means of relieving the wants of others; and therefore I cannot affect to despise them. I must persuade my brother Murad to share them with me, and to forget his misfortunes : I shall then think myself completely happy. As to the sultana's looking-glass, and your broken vase, my dear brother," continued Saladin, " we must think of some means — "

" Think no more of the sultana's looking-glass, or of the broken vase," exclaimed the sultan, throwing aside his merchant's habit, and showing beneath it his own imperial vest. "Saladin, I rejoice to have heard, from your own lips, the history of your life. I acknowledge, vizier, I have been in the wrong, in our argument," continued the sultan, turning to his vizier. "I acknowledge that the histories of Saladin the Lucky and Murad the Unlucky favor your opinion, that prudence has more influence than chance in human affairs. The success and happiness of Saladin seem to me to have arisen from his prudence: by that prudence, Constantinople has been saved from flames, and from the plague. Had Murad possessed his brother's discretion, he would not have been on the point of losing his head, for selling rolls which he did not bake: he would not have been kicked by a mule, or bastinadoed for finding a ring: he would not have been robbed by one party of soldiers, or shot by another: he would not have been lost in a desert, or cheated by a Jew; he would not have set a ship on fire; nor would he have caught the plague, and spread it through Grand Cairo: he would not have run my sultana's looking-glass through the body, instead of a robber: he would not have believed that the fate of his life depended on certain verses on a china vase: nor would he, at last, have broken this precious talisman, by washing it with hot water. Henceforward, let Murad the Unlucky be named Murad the Imprudent: let Saladin preserve the surname he merits, and be henceforth called Saladin the Prudent."

So spake the sultan, who, unlike the generality of monarchs, could bear to find himself in the wrong; and could discover his vizier to be in the right, without cutting off his head. History further informs us that the sultan offered to make Saladin a pacha, and to commit to him the government of a province; but Saladin the Prudent declined this honor, saying he had no ambition, was perfectly happy in his present situation, and that, when this was the case, it would be folly to change, because no one can be more than happy. What further adventures befell Murad the Imprudent are not recorded; it is known only that he became a daily visitor to the *Teriaky;* and that he died a martyr to the immoderate use of opium.

THE CHILDREN OF THE PUBLIC.

BY EDWARD EVERETT HALE.

I.

MY LIFE TO ITS CRISIS.

EW-YORKERS of to-day see so many processions, and live through so many sensations, and hurrah for so many heroes in every year, that it is only the oldest of fogies who tells you of the triumphant procession of steamboats which, in the year 1824, welcomed General Lafayette on his arrival from his tour through the country he had so nobly served. But, if the reader wishes to lengthen out this story, he may button the next silver-gray friend he meets, and ask him to tell of the broken English and broken French of the Marquis, of Levasseur, and the rest of them; of the enthusiasm of the people and the readiness of the visitors, and he will please bear in mind that of all that am I.

For it so happened that on the morning when, for want of better lions to show, the mayor and governor and the rest of them took the Marquis and his secretary, and the rest of them, to see the orphan asylum in Deering Street, — as they passed into the first ward, after having had "a little refreshment" in the managers' room, Sally Eaton, the head nurse, dropped the first courtesy to them, and Sally Eaton, as it happened, held me screaming in her arms. I had been sent to the asylum that morning with a paper pinned to my bib, which said my name was Felix Carter.

"Eet ees verra fine," said the Marquis, smiling blandly.

"Ràvissant!" said Levasseur, and he dropped a five-franc piece into Sally Eaton's hand. And so the procession of exhibiting managers talking bad French, and of exhibited Frenchmen talking bad English, passed on; all but good old Elkanah Ogden, — God bless him! — who happened to have come there with the governor's party, and who loitered a minute to talk with Sally Eaton about me.

Years afterwards she told me how the old man kissed me, how his eyes watered when he asked my story, how she told again of the moment when I was heard screaming on the doorstep, and how she offered to go and bring the paper which had been pinned to my bib. But the old man said it was no matter, — "only we would have called him Marquis," said he, "if his name was not provided for him. We must not leave him here," he said; "he shall grow up a farmer's lad, and not a little cockney." And so, instead of going the grand round of infirmaries, kitchens, bakeries, and dormitories with the rest, the good old soul went back into the managers' room, and wrote at the moment a letter to John Myers, who took care of his wild land in St. Lawrence County for him, to ask him if Mrs. Myers would not bring up an orphan baby by hand for him; and if, both together, they would not train this baby till he said "Stop"; if, on the other hand, he allowed them, in the yearly account, a hundred dollars each year for the charge.

Anybody who knows how far a hundred dollars goes in the backwoods, in St. Lawrence County, will know that any settler would be glad to take a ward so recommended. Anybody who knew Betsy Myers as well as old Elkanah Ogden did, would know she would have taken any orphan brought to her door, even if he were not recommended at all.

So it happened, thanks to Lafayette and the city council! that I had not been a "Child of the Public" a day, before, in its great, clumsy, liberal way, it had provided for me. I owed my healthy, happy home of the next fourteen years in the wilderness to those marvellous habits, which I should else call absurd, with which we lionize strangers. Because our hospitals and poorhouses are the largest buildings we have, we entertain the Prince of Wales and Jenny Lind alike, by showing them crazy people and paupers. Easy enough to laugh at is the display; but if, dear Public, it happen that by such a habit you ventilate your Bridewell or your Bedlam, is not the ventilation, perhaps, a compensation for the absurdity? I do not know if Lafayette was any the better for his seeing the Deering Street Asylum; but I do know I was.

This is no history of my life. It is only an illustration of one of its principles. I have no anecdotes of wilderness life to tell, and no sketch of the lovely rugged traits of John and Betsy Myers, — my real father and mother. I have no quest for the pretended parents, who threw me away in my babyhood, to record. They closed accounts with me when they left me on the asylum steps, and I with them. I grew up with such schooling as the public gave, — ten weeks in winter always, and ten in summer, till I was big enough to work on the farm, — better periods of schools, I hold, than on the modern systems. Mr. Ogden I never saw. Regularly he allowed for me the hundred a year till I was nine years old, and then suddenly he died, as the reader perhaps knows. But John Myers kept me as his son, none the less. I knew no change until, when I was fourteen, he thought it time for me to see the world, and sent me to what, in those days, was called a "Manual-Labor School."

There was a theory coming up in those days, wholly unfounded in physiology, that if a man worked five hours with his hands, he could study better in the next five. It is all nonsense. Exhaustion is exhaustion ; and if you exhaust a vessel by one stopcock, nothing is gained or saved by closing that and opening another. The old up-country theory is the true one. Study ten weeks and chop wood fifteen ; study ten more and harvest fifteen. But the "Manual-Labor School" offered itself for really no pay, only John Myers and I carried over, I remember, a dozen barrels of potatoes when I went there with my books. The school was kept at Roscius, and if I would work in the carpenter's shop and on the school farm five hours, why they would feed me and teach me all they knew in what I had of the day beside.

"Felix," said John, as he left me, "I do not suppose this is the best school in the world, unless you make it so. But I do suppose you can make it so. If you and I went whining about, looking for the best school in the world, and for somebody to pay your way through it, I should die, and you would lose your voice with whining, and we should not find one after all. This is what the public happens to provide for you and me. We won't look a gift-horse in the mouth. Get on his back, Felix ; groom him well as you can when you stop, feed him when you can, and at all events water him well and take care of him well. My last advice to you, Felix, is to take what is offered you, and never complain because nobody offers more."

Those words are to be cut on my seal-ring, if I ever have one, and if Dr. Anthon or Professor Webster will put them into short enough Latin for me. That is the motto of the "Children of the Public."

John Myers died before that term was out. And my more than mother, Betsy, went back to her friends in Maine. After the funeral I never saw them more. How I lived from that moment to what Fausta and I call the Crisis is nobody's concern. I worked in the shop at the school, or on the farm. Afterwards I taught school in neighboring districts. I never bought a ticket in a lottery or a raffle. But whenever there was a chance to do an honest stroke of work, I did it. I have walked fifteen miles at night to carry an election return to the "Tribune's" agent at Gouverneur. I have turned out in the snow to break open the road when the supervisor could not find another man in the township.

When Sartain started his magazine, I wrote an essay in competition for his premiums, and the essay earned its hundred dollars. When the managers of the "Orphan Home," in Baltimore, offered their prizes for papers on bad boys, I wrote for one of them, and that helped me on four hard months. There was no luck in those things. I needed the money, and I put my hook into the pork-barrel, — that is, I trusted the Public. I never had but one stroke of luck in my life. I wanted a new pair of boots badly. I was going to walk to Albany, to work in the State library on the history of the Six Nations, which had an interest for me. I did not have a dollar. Just then there passed Congress the bill dividing the surplus revenue. The State of New York received two or three millions, and divided it among the counties. The county of St. Lawrence divided it among the townships, and the township of Roscius divided it among the voters. Two dollars and sixty cents of Uncle Sam's money came to me, and with that money on my feet I walked to Albany. That I call luck! How many fools had to assent in an absurdity before I could study the history of the Six Nations!

But one instance told in detail is better than a thousand told in general, for the illustration of a principle. So I will detain you no longer from the history of what Fausta and I call The Crisis.

II.

THE CRISIS.

I was at work as a veneerer in a piano-forte factory at Attica, when some tariff or other was passed or repealed; there came a great financial explosion, and our boss, among the rest, failed. He owed us all six months' wages, and we were all very poor and very blue. Jonathan Whittemore — a real good fellow, who used to cover the hammers with leather — came to me the day the shop was closed, and told me he was going to take the chance to go to Europe. He was going to the Musical Conservatory at Leipsic, if he could. He would work his passage out as a stoker. He would wash himself for three or four days at Bremen, and then get work, if he could, with Voightlander or Von Hammer till he could enter the Conservatory. By way of preparation for this he wanted me to sell him my Adler's German Dictionary.

"I 've nothing to give you for it, Felix, but this foolish thing, — it is one of Burrham's tickets, — which I bought in a frolic the night of our sleigh-ride. I 'll transfer it to you."

I told Jonathan he might have the dictionary and welcome. He was doing a sensible thing, and he would use it twenty times as much as I should. As for the ticket, he had better keep it. I did not want it. But I saw he would feel better if I took it, — so he indorsed it to me.

Now the reader must know that this Burrham was a man who had got hold of one corner of the idea of what the Public could do for its children. He had found out that there were a thousand people who would be glad to make the tour of the mountains and the lakes every summer if they could do it for half price. He found out that the railroad companies were glad enough to put the price down if they could be sure of the thousand people. He mediated between the two, and so "cheap excursions" came into being. They are one of the gifts the Public gives its children. Rising from step to step, Burrham had, just before the great financial crisis, conceived the idea of a great cheap combination, in which everybody was to receive a magazine for a year and a cyclopædia, both at half price; and not only so, but the money that was gained in the combination was to be given by lot to two ticket-holders, one a man and one a woman, for their dowry in marriage. I dare say the reader remembers the prospectus. It savors too much of the modern "Gift Enterprise" to be reprinted in full; but it had this honest element, that everybody got more than he could get for his money in retail. I have my magazine, the old "Boston Miscellany," to this day, and I just now looked out Levasseur's name in my cyclopædia; and, as you will see, I have reason to know that all the other subscribers got theirs.

One of the tickets for these books, for which Whittemore had given five good dollars, was what he gave to me for my dictionary. And so we parted. I loitered at Attica, hoping for a place where I could put in my oar. But my hand was out at teaching, and in a time when all the world's veneers of different kinds were ripping off, nobody wanted me to put on more of my kind, — so that my cash ran low. I would not go in debt, — that is a thing I never did. More honest, I say, to go to the poorhouse, and make the Public care for its child there, than to borrow what you cannot pay. But I did not come quite to that, as you shall see.

I was counting up my money one night, — and it was easily done, — when I observed that the date on this

Burrham order was the 15th of October, and it occurred
to me that it was not quite a fortnight before those books
were to be delivered. They were to be delivered at
Castle Garden, at New York; and the thought struck
me that I might go to New York, try my chance there
for work, and at least see the city, which I had never
seen, and get my cyclopædia and magazine. It was the
least offer the Public ever made to me; but just then the
Public was in a collapse, and the least was better than
nothing. The plan of so long a journey was Quixotic
enough, and I hesitated about it a good deal. Finally I
came to this resolve: I would start in the morning to
walk to the lock-station at Brockport on the canal. If a
boat passed that night where they would give me my
fare for any work I could do for them, I would go to
Albany. If not, I would walk back to Lockport the
next day, and try my fortune there. This gave me, for
my first day's enterprise, a foot journey of about twenty-
five miles. It was out of the question, with my finances,
for me to think of compassing the train.

Every point of life is a pivot on which turns the whole
action of our after-lives; and so, indeed, of the after-
lives of the whole world. But we are so purblind that
we only see this of certain special enterprises and endeavors, which we therefore call critical. I am sure I
see it of that twenty-five miles of fresh autumnal walking.
I was in tip-top spirits. I found the air all oxygen, and
everything "all right." I did not loiter, and I did not
hurry. I swung along with the feeling that every nerve
and muscle drew, as in the trades a sailor feels of every
rope and sail. And so I was not tired, not thirsty, till

the brook appeared where I was to drink; nor hungry
till twelve o'clock came, when I was to dine. I called
myself, as I walked, "The Child of Good Fortune," because the sun was on my right quarter, as the sun should
be when you walk, because the rain of yesterday had laid
the dust for me, and the frost of yesterday had painted
the hills for me, and the northwest wind cooled the air
for me. I came to Wilkie's Cross-Roads just in time to
meet the Claremont baker and buy my dinner loaf of
him. And when my walk was nearly done, I came out
on the low bridge at Sewell's, which is a drawbridge,
just before they raised it for a passing boat, instead of
the moment after. Because I was all right I felt myself
and called myself "The Child of Good Fortune." Dear
reader, in a world made by a loving Father, we are
all of us children of good fortune, if we only have wit
enough to find it out, as we stroll along.

The last stroke of good fortune which that day had for
me was the solution of my question whether or no I
would go to Babylon. I was to go if any good-natured
boatman would take me. This is a question, Mr. Millionnaire, more doubtful to those who have not drawn
their dividends than to those who have. As I came
down the village street at Brockport, I could see the
horses of a boat bound eastward, led along from level to
level at the last lock; and, in spite of my determination
not to hurry, I put myself on the long, loping trot which
the St. Regis Indians taught me, that I might overhaul
this boat before she got under way at her new speed. I
came out on the upper gate of the last lock just as she
passed out from the lower gate. The horses were just

put on, and a reckless boy gave them their first blow after two hours of rest and corn. As the heavy boat started off under the new motion, I saw, and her skipper saw at the same instant, that a long new tow-rope of his, which had lain coiled on deck, was suddenly flying out to its full length. The outer end of it had been carried upon the lock-side by some chance or blunder, and there some idle loafer had thrown the looped bight of it over a hawser-post. The loafers on the lock saw, as I did, that the rope was running out, and at the call of the skipper one of them condescended to throw the loop overboard, but he did it so carelessly that the lazy rope rolled over into the lock, and the loop caught on one of the valve-irons of the upper gate. The whole was the business of an instant, of course. But the poor skipper saw, what we did not, that the coil of the rope on deck was foul, and so entangled round his long tiller, that ten seconds would do one of three things, — they would snap his new rope in two, which was a trifle, or they would wrench his tiller-head off the rudder, which would cost him an hour to mend, or they would upset those two horses, at this instant on a trot, and put into the canal the rowdy youngster who had started them. It was this complex certainty which gave fire to the double cries which he addressed aft to us on the lock, and forward to the magnet boy, whose indifferent intelligence at that moment drew him along.

I was stepping upon the gate-head to walk across it. It took but an instant, not nearly all the ten seconds, to swing down by my arms into the lock, keeping myself hanging by my hands, to catch with my right foot the bight of the rope and lift it off the treacherous iron, to kick the whole into the water, and then to scramble up the wet lock-side again. I got a little wet, but that was nothing. I ran down the tow-path, beckoned to the skipper, who sheered his boat up to the shore, and I jumped on board.

At that moment, reader, Fausta was sitting in a yellow chair on the deck of that musty old boat, crocheting from a pattern in " Godey's Lady's Book. I remember it as I remember my breakfast of this morning. Not that I fell in love with her, nor did I fall in love with my breakfast; but I knew she was there. And that was the first time I ever saw her. It is many years since, and I have seen her every day from that evening to this evening. But I had then no business with her. My affair was with him whom I have called the skipper, by way of adapting this fresh-water narrative to ears accustomed to Marryat and Tom Cringle. I told him that I had to go to New York; that I had not time to walk, and had not money to pay; that I should like to work my passage to Troy, if there were any way in which I could; and to ask him this I had come on board.

" Waal," said the skipper, " 't ain't much that is to be done, and Zekiel and I calc'late to do most of that; and there's that blamed boy beside — "

This adjective " blamed " is the virtuous oath by which simple people, who are improving their habits, cure themselves of a stronger epithet, as men take to flag-root who are abandoning tobacco.

" He ain't good for nothin', as you see," continued

the skipper meditatively, "and you air, anybody can see that," he added. "Ef you 've mind to come to Albany, you can have your vittles, poor enough they are too; and ef you are willing to ride sometimes, you can ride. I guess where there 's room for three in the bunks there 's room for four. 'T ain't everybody would have cast off that blamed hawser-rope as neat as you did."

From which last remark I inferred, what I learned as a certainty as we travelled farther, that but for the timely assistance I had rendered him I should have plead for my passage in vain.

This was my introduction to Fausta. That is to say, she heard the whole of the conversation. The formal introduction, which is omitted in no circle of American life to which I have ever been admitted, took place at tea half an hour after, when Mrs. Grills, who always voyaged with her husband, brought in the flapjacks from the kitchen. "Miss Jones," said Grills, as I came into the meal, leaving Zekiel at the tiller, — "Miss Jones, this is a young man who is going to Albany. I don't rightly know how to call your name, sir." I said my name was Carter. Then he said, "Mr. Carter, this is Miss Jones. Mrs. Grills, Mr. Carter. Mr. Carter, Mrs. Grills. She is my wife." And so our *partie carrée* was established for the voyage.

In these days there are few people who know that a journey on a canal is the pleasantest journey in the world. A canal has to go through fine scenery. It cannot exist unless it follow through the valley of a stream. The movement is so easy that, with your eyes shut, you do not know you move. The route is so direct, that

when you are once shielded from the sun, you are safe
for hours. You draw, you read, you write, or you sew,
crochet, or knit. You play on your flute or your guitar,
without one hint of inconvenience. At a "low bridge"
you duck your head lest you lose your hat, — and that
reminder teaches you that you are human. You are glad
to know this, and you laugh at the memento. For the
rest of the time you journey, if you are "all right"
within, in Elysium.

I rode one of those horses perhaps two or three hours
a day. At locks I made myself generally useful. At
night I walked the deck till one o'clock, with my pipe or
without it, to keep guard against the lock-thieves. The
skipper asked me sometimes, after he found I could "cipher," to disentangle some of the knots in his bills of
lading for him. But all this made but a little inroad in
those lovely autumn days, and for the eight days that we
glided along, — there is one blessed level which is seventy miles long, — I spent most of my time with Fausta.
We walked together on the tow-path to get our appetites
for dinner and for supper. At sunrise I always made a
cruise inland, and collected the gentians and black alder-
berries and colored leaves, with which she dressed Mrs.
Grill's table. She took an interest in my wretched
sketch-book; and though she did not and does not draw
well, she did show me how to spread an even tint, which
I never knew before. I was working up my French.
She knew about as much and as little as I did, and we
read Mad Reybaud's Clementine together, guessing at
the hard words, because we had no dictionary.

Dear old Grill offered to talk French at table, and we

tried it for a few days. But it proved he picked up his pronunciation at St. Catherine's, among the boatmen there, and he would say *shwo* for "horses," where the book said *chevaux*. Our talk, on the other hand, was not Parisian, — but it was not Catherinian, — and we subsided into English again.

So sped along these blessed eight days. I told Fausta thus much of my story, that I was going to seek my fortune in New York. She, of course, knew nothing of me but what she saw, and she told me nothing of her story.

But I was very sorry when we came into the basin at Troy, for I knew then that in all reason I must take the steamboat down. And I was very glad — I have seldom in my life been so glad — when I found that she also was going to New York immediately. She accepted, very pleasantly, my offer to carry her trunk to the Isaac Newton for her, and to act as her escort to the city. For me, my trunk,

> " in danger tried,"
> Swung in my hand, — " nor left my side."

My earthly possessions were few anywhere. I had left at Attica most of what they were. Through the voyage I had been man enough to heep on a working-gear fit for a workman's duty. And old Grills had not yet grace enough to keep his boat still on Sunday. How one remembers little things! I can remember each touch of the toilet, as, in that corner of a dark cuddy where I had shared "Zekiel's" bunk with him, I dressed myself with one of my two white shirts, and with the change of raiment which had been tight squeezed in my portmanteau. The old overcoat was the best part of it, as in a finite world it often is. I sold my felt hat to Zekiel, and appeared with a light travelling-cap. I do not know how Fausta liked my metamorphosis. I only know that, like butterflies, for a day or two after they go through theirs, I felt decidedly cold.

As Carter, the canal man, I had carried Fausta's trunk on board. As Mr. Carter; I gave her my arm, led her to the gangway of the Newton, took her passage and mine, and afterwards walked and sat through the splendid moonlight of the first four hours down the river.

Miss Joues determined that evening to breakfast on the boat. Be it observed that I did not then know her by any other name. She was to go to an aunt's house, and she knew that if she left the boat on its early arrival in New York, she would disturb that lady by a premature ringing at her bell. I had no reason for haste, as the reader knows. The distribution of the cyclopædias was not to take place till the next day, and that absurd trifle was the only distinct excuse I had to myself for being in New York at all. I asked Miss Jones, therefore, if I might not be her escort still to her aunt's house. I had said it would be hard to break off our pleasant journey before I had seen where she lived, and I thought she seemed relieved to know that she should not be wholly a stranger on her arrival. It was clear enough that her aunt would send no one to meet her.

These preliminaries adjusted, we parted to our respective cabins. And when, the next morning, at that unearthly hour demanded by Philadelphia trains and other exigencies, the Newton made her dock, I rejoiced that breakfast was not till seven o'clock, that I had two hours more of the berth, which was luxury compared to Zekiel's bunk, — I turned upon my other side and slept on.

Sorry enough for that morning nap was I for the next thirty-six hours. For when I went on deck, and sent in the stewardess to tell Miss Jones that I was waiting for her, and then took from her the check for her trunk, I woke to the misery of finding that, in that treacherous two hours, some pirate from the pier had stepped on board, had seized the waiting trunk, left almost alone, while the baggage-master's back was turned, and that, to a certainty, it was lost. I did not return to Fausta with this story till the breakfast-bell had long passed and the breakfast was very cold. I did not then tell it to her till I had seen her eat her breakfast with an appetite much better than mine. I had already offered up stairs the largest reward to anybody who would bring it back which my scanty purse would pay. I had spoken to the clerk, who had sent for a policeman. I could do nothing more, and I did not choose to ruin her chop and coffee by ill-timed news. The officer came before breakfast was over, and called me from table.

On the whole, his business-like way encouraged me. He had some clews which I had not thought possible. It was not unlikely that they should pounce on the trunk before it was broken open. I gave him a written description of its marks; and when he civilly asked if "my lady" would give some description of any books or other articles within, I readily promised that I would call with such a description at the police station. Somewhat encouraged, I returned to Miss Jones, and, when I led her from the breakfast-table, told her of her misfortune. I took all shame to myself for my own carelessness, to which I attributed the loss. But I told her all that the officer had said to me, and that I hoped to bring her the trunk at her aunt's before the day was over.

Fausta took my news, however, with a start which frightened me. All her money, but a shilling or two, was in the trunk. To place money in trunks is a weakness of the female mind which I have nowhere seen accounted for. Worse than this, though, — as appeared after a moment's examination of her travelling-*sac*,— her portfolio in the trunk contained the letter of the aunt whom she came to visit, giving her her address in the city. To this address she had no other clew but that her aunt was Mrs. Mary Mason, had married a few years before a merchant named Mason, whom Miss Jones had never seen, and of whose name and business this was all she knew. They lived in a numbered street, but whether it was Fourth Street, or Fifty-fourth, or One Hundred and Twenty-fourth, or whether it was something between, the poor child had no idea. She had put up the letter carefully, but had never thought of the importance of the address. Besides this aunt, she knew no human being in New York.

" Child of the Public," I said to myself, " what do you do now ? " I had appealed to my great patron in sending for the officer, and on the whole I felt that my sovereign had been gracious to me, if not yet hopeful. But now I must rub my lamp again, and ask the genie where the

unknown Mason lived. The genie of course suggested
the Directory, and I ran for it to the clerk's office. But
as we were toiling down the pages of "Masons," and
had written off thirteen or fourteen who lived in numbered streets, Fausta started, looked back at the preface
and its date, flung down her pencil in the only abandon-
ment of dismay in which I ever saw her, and cried "First
of May! They were abroad until May. They have been
abroad since the day they were married!" So that
genie had to put his glories into his pocket, and carry his
Directory back to the office again.

The natural thing to propose was, that I should find
for Miss Jones a respectable boarding-house, and that
she should remain there until her trunk was found, or
till she could write to friends who had this fatal address,
and receive an answer. But here she hesitated. She
hardly liked to explain why, — did not explain wholly.
But she did not say that she had no friends who knew
this address. She had but few relations in the world,
and her aunt had communicated with her alone since she
came from Europe. As for the boarding-house, "I had
rather look for work," she said bravely. "I have never
promised to pay money when I did not know how to obtain it; and that" — and here she took out fifty or sixty
cents from her purse — "and that is all now. In respectable boarding-houses, when people come without lug-
gage, they are apt to ask for an advance. Or, at least,"
she added, with some pride, "I am apt to offer it."

I hastened to ask her to take all my little store; but I
had to own that I had not two dollars. I was sure,
however, that my overcoat and the dress-suit I wore

would avail me something, if I thrust them boldly up some spout. I was sure that I should be at work within a day or two. At all events, I was certain of the cyclopædia the next day. That should go to old Gowan's, — in Fulton Street it was then, — "the moral centre of the intellectual world," in the hour I got it. And at this moment, for the first time, the thought crossed me, "If mine could only be the name drawn, so that that foolish $ 5,000 should fall to me. In that case I felt that Fausta might live in "a respectable boarding-house" till she died. Of this, of course, I said nothing, only that she was welcome to my poor dollar and a half, and that I should receive the next day some more money that was due me.

"You forget, Mr. Carter," replied Fausta, as proudly as before, — "you forget that I cannot borrow of you any more than of a boarding-house-keeper. I never borrow. Please God, I never will. It must be," she added, "that in a Christian city like this there is some respectable and fit arrangement made for travellers who find themselves where I am. What that provision is I do not know : but I will find out what it is before this sun goes down."

I paused a moment before I replied. If I had been fascinated by this lovely girl before, I now bowed in respect before her dignity and resolution ; and, with my sympathy, there was a delicious throb of self-respect united, when I heard her lay down so simply, as principles of her life, two principles on which I had always myself tried to live. The half-expressed habits of my boyhood and youth were now uttered for me as axioms

7 *

by lips which I knew could speak nothing but right and truth.

I paused a moment. I stumbled a little as I expressed my regret that she would not let me help her, — joined with my certainty that she was in the right in refusing, — and then, in the only stiff speech I ever made to her, I said : —

"I am the 'Child of the Public.' If you ever hear my story, you will say so too. At the least, I can claim this, that I have a right to help you in your quest as to the way in which the public will help you. Thus far I am clearly the officer in his suite to whom he has intrusted you. Are you ready, then, to go on shore?"

Fausta looked around on that forlorn ladies' saloon, as if it were the last link holding her to her old safe world.

> "Looked upon skylight, lamp, and chain,
>   As what she ne'er might see again."

Then she looked right through me; and if there had been one mean thought in me at that minute, she would have seen the viper. Then she said sadly, —

"I have perfect confidence in you, though people would say we were strangers. Let us go."

And we left the boat together. We declined the invitations of the noisy hackmen, and walked slowly to Broadway.

We stopped at the station-house for that district, and to the attentive chief Fausta herself described those contents of her trunk which she thought would be most easily detected, if offered for sale. Her mother's Bible, at which the chief shook his head; Bibles, alas! brought nothing at the shops; a soldier's medal, such as were given as target prizes by the Montgomery regiment, and a little silver canteen, marked with the device of the same regiment, seemed to him better worthy of note. Her portfolio was wrought with a cipher, and she explained to him that she was most eager that this should be recovered. The pocket-book contained more than one hundred dollars, which she described, but he shook his head here, and gave her but little hope of that, if the trunk were once opened. His chief hope was for this morning.

"And where shall we send to you then, madam?" said he.

I had been proud, as if it were my merit, of the impression Fausta had made upon the officer, in her quiet, simple, lady-like dress and manner. For myself, I thought that one slip of pretence in my dress or bearing, a scrap of gold or of pinchbeck, would have ruined both of us in our appeal. But, fortunately, I did not disgrace her, and the man looked at her as if he expected her to say, "Fourteenth Street." What would she say?

"That depends upon what the time will be. Mr. Carter will call at noon, and will let you know."

We bowed, and were gone. In an instant more she begged my pardon, almost with tears; but I told her that if she also had been a "Child of the Public," she could not more fitly have spoken to one of her father's officers. I begged her to use me as her protector, and not to apologize again. Then we laid out the plans which we followed out that day.

The officer's manner had reassured her, and I succeeded in persuading her that it was certain we should have the trunk at noon. How much better to wait, at least so far, before she entered on any of the enterprises of which she talked so coolly, as of offering herself as a nursery-girl, or as a milliner, to whoever would employ her, if only she could thus secure an honest home till money or till aunt were found. Once persuaded that we were safe from this Quixotism, I told her that we must go on, as we did on the canal, and first we must take our constitutional walk for two hours.

"At least," she said, "our good papa, the Public, gives us wonderful sights to see, and good walking to our feet, as a better Father has given us this heavenly sky and this bracing air."

And with those words the last heaviness of despondency left her face for that day. And we plunged into the delicious adventure of exploring a new city, staring into windows as only strangers can, revelling in print-shops as only they do, really seeing the fine buildings as residents always forget to do, and laying up, in short, with those streets, nearly all the associations which to this day we have with them.

Two hours of this tired us with walking, of course. I do not know what she meant to do next; but at ten I said, "Time for French, Miss Jones." "Ah oui," said she, "mais où?" and I had calculated my distances, and led her at once into Lafayette Place; and, in a moment, pushed open the door of the Astor Library, led her up the main stairway, and said, "This is what the Public provides for his children when they have to study."

"This is the Astor," said she, delighted. "And we

are all right, as you say, here?" Then she saw that our entrance excited no surprise among the few readers, men and women, who were beginning to assemble.

We took our seats at an unoccupied table, and began to revel in the luxuries for which we had only to ask that we might enjoy. I had a little memorandum of books which I had been waiting to see. She needed none; but looked for one and another, and yet another, and between us we kept the attendant well in motion. A pleasant thing to me to be finding out her thorough-bred tastes and lines of work, and I was happy enough to interest her in some of my pet readings; and, of course, for she was a woman, to get quick hints which had never dawned on me before. A very short hour and a half we spent there before I went to the station-house again. I went very quickly, I returned to her very slowly.

The trunk was not found. But they were now quite sure they were on its track. They felt certain it had been carried from pier to pier and taken back up the river. Nor was it hopeless to follow it. The particular rascal who was supposed to have it would certainly stop either at Piermont or at Newburg. They had telegraphed to both places, and were in time for both. " The day boat, sir, will bring your lady's trunk, and will bring me Rowdy Rob, too, I hope," said the officer. But at the same moment, as he rang his bell, he learned that no despatch had yet been received from either of the places named. I did not feel so certain as he did.

But Fausta showed no discomfort as I told my news.

"Thus far," said she, "the Public serves me well. I will borrow no trouble by want of faith." And I, — as Dante would say, — and I, to her, "Will you let me remind you, then, that at one we dine; that Mrs. Grills is now placing the salt-pork upon the cabin table, and Mr. Grills asking the blessing; and, as this is the only day when I can have the honor of your company, will you let me show you how a Child of the Public dines, when his finances are low?"

Fausta laughed, and said again, less tragically than before, "I have perfect confidence in you," — little thinking how she started my blood with the words; but this time, as if in token, she let me take her hand upon my arm, as we walked down the street together.

If we had been snobs, or even if I had been one, I should have taken her to Taylor's, and have spent all the money I had on such a luncheon as neither of us had ever eaten before. Whatever else I am, I am not a snob of that sort. I show my colors. I led her into a little cross-street which I had noticed in our erratic morning pilgrimage. We stopped at a German baker's. I bade her sit down at the neat marble table, and I bought two rolls. She declined lager, which I offered her in fun. We took water instead, and we had dined, and had paid two cents for our meal, and had had a very merry dinner, too, when the clock struck two.

"And now, Mr. Carter," said she, "I will steal no more of your day. You did not come to New York to escort lone damsels to the Astor Library or to dinner. Nor did I come only to see the lions or to read French. I insist on your going to your affairs, and leaving me to

mine. If you will meet me at the Library half an hour
before it closes, I will thank you; till then," with a
tragedy shake of the hand, and a merry laugh, "adieu!"

I knew very well that no harm could happen to her in
two hours of an autumn afternoon. I was not sorry for
her *congé*, for it gave me an opportunity to follow my
own plans. I stopped at one or two cabinet-makers, and
talked with the "jours" about work, that I might tell
her with truth that I had been in search of it; then
I sedulously began on calling upon every man I could
reach named Mason. O, how often I went through one
phase or another of this colloquy : —

"Is Mr. Mason in ? "

"That's my name, sir."

"Can you give me the address of Mr. Mason who
returned from Europe last May ? "

"Know no such person, sir."

The reader can imagine how many forms this dialogue could be repeated in, before, as I wrought my way
through a long line of dry-goods cases to a distant
counting-room, I heard some one in it say, "No, madam, I know no such person as you describe"; and from
the recess Fausta emerged and met me. Her plan for
the afternoon had been the same with mine. We laughed
as we detected each other ; then I told her she had had
quite enough of this, that it was time she should rest, and
took her, *nolens volens*, into the ladies' parlor of the St.
Nicholas, and bade her wait there through the twilight,
with my copy of Clementine, till I should return from
the police-station. If the reader has ever waited in such
a place for some one to come and attend to him, he will

understand that nobody will be apt to molest him when
he has not asked for attention.

Two hours I left Fausta in the rocking-chair, which
there the Public had provided for her. Then I returned,
sadly enough. No tidings of Rowdy Rob, none of
trunk, Bible, money, letter, medal, or anything. Still
was my district sergeant hopeful, and, as always, re-
spectful. But I was hopeless this time, and I knew that
the next day Fausta would be plunging into the war
with intelligence-houses and advertisements. For the
night, I was determined that she should spend it in my
ideal "respectable boarding-house." On my way down
town, I stopped in at one or two shops to make inquiries,
and satisfied myself where I would take her. Still I
thought it wisest that we should go after tea; and another cross-street baker, and another pair of rolls, and
another tap at the Croton, provided that repast for us.
Then I told Fausta of the respectable boarding-house,
and that she must go there. She did not say no. But
she did say she would rather not spend the evening
there. "There must be some place open for us," said
she. "There! there is a church-bell! The church is
always home. Let us come there."

So to "evening meeting" we went, startling the sexton by arriving an hour early. If there were any who
wondered what was the use of that Wednesday-evening
service, we did not. In a dark gallery pew we sat, she
at one end, I at the other; and, if the whole truth be
told, each of us fell asleep at once, and slept till the
heavy organ tones taught us that the service had begun.
A hundred or more people had straggled in then, and the

preacher, good soul, he took for his text, "Doth not God care for the ravens?" I cannot describe the ineffable feeling of home that came over me in that dark pew of that old church. I had never been in so large a church before. I had never heard so heavy an organ before. Perhaps I had heard better preaching, but never any that came to my occasions more. But it was none of these things which moved me. It was the fact that we were just where we had a right to be. No impudent waiter could ask us why we were sitting there, nor any petulant policeman propose that we should push on. It was God's house, and, because his, it was his children's.

All this feeling of repose grew upon me, and, as it proved, upon Fausta also. For when the service was ended, and I ventured to ask her whether she also had this sense of home and rest, she assented so eagerly, that I proposed, though with hesitation, a notion which had crossed me, that I should leave her there.

"I cannot think," I said, "of any possible harm that could come to you before morning."

"Do you know, I had thought of that very same thing, but I did not dare tell you," she said.

Was not I glad that she had considered me her keeper! But I only said, "At the 'respectable boarding-house' you might be annoyed by questions."

"And no one will speak to me here. I know that from Goody Two-Shoes."

"I will be here," said I, "at sunrise in the morning." And so I bade her good by, insisting on leaving in the pew my own great-coat. I knew she might need it before morning. I walked out as the sexton closed the

K

door below on the last of the down-stairs worshippers.
He passed along the aisles below, with his long poker
which screwed down the gas. I saw at once that he had
no intent of exploring the galleries. But I loitered outside till I saw him lock the doors and depart; and then,
happy in the thought that Miss Jones was in the safest
place in New York, — as comfortable as she was the
night before, and much more comfortable than she had
been any night upon the canal, — I went in search of my
own lodging.

"To the respectable boarding-house?"

Not a bit, reader. I had no shillings for respectable
or disrespectable boarding - houses. I asked the first
policeman where his district station was. I went into
its office, and told the captain that I was green in the
city; had got no work and no money. In truth, I had
left my purse in Miss Jones's charge, and a five-cent
piece, which I showed the chief, was all I had. He said
no word but to bid me go up two flights and turn into
the first bunk I found. I did so; and in five minutes
was asleep in a better bed than I had slept in for nine
days.

That was what the Public did for me that night. I,
too, was safe!

I am making this story too long. But with that night
and its anxieties the end has come. At sunrise I rose
and made my easy toilet. I bought and ate my roll, —
varying the brand from yesterday's. I bought another,
with a lump of butter, and an orange, for Fausta. I left
my portmanteau at the station, while I rushed to the
sexton's house, told his wife I had left my gloves in

church the night before, — as was the truth, — and easily obtained from her the keys. In a moment I was in the vestibule, — locked in, — was in the gallery, and there found Fausta, just awake, as she declared, from a comfortable night, reading her morning lesson in the Bible, and sure, she said, that I should soon appear. Nor ghost, nor wraith, had visited her. I spread for her a brown paper table-cloth on the table in the vestibule. I laid out her breakfast for her, called her, and wondered at her toilet. How is it that women always make themselves appear as neat and finished as if there were no conflict, dust, or wrinkle in the world?

[Here Fausta adds, in this manuscript, a parenthesis, to say that she folded her undersleeves neatly, and her collar, before she slept, and put them between the cushions, upon which she slept. In the morning they had been pressed — without a sad-iron.]

She finished her repast. I opened the church-door for five minutes. She passed out when she had enough examined the monuments, and at a respectable distance I followed her. We joined each other, and took our accustomed morning walk; but then she resolutely said, "Good by," for the day. She would find work before night, — work and a home. And I must do the same. Only when I pressed her to let me know of her success, she said she would meet me at the Astor Library just before it closed. No, she would not take my money. Enough, that for twenty-four hours she had been my guest. When she had found her aunt and told her the story, they should insist on repaying this hospitality. Hospitality, dear reader, which I had dispensed at the

charge of six cents. Have you ever treated Miranda for
a day and found the charge so low? When I urged
other assistance she said resolutely, "No." In fact, she
had already made an appointment at two, she said, and
she must not waste the day.

I also had an appointment at two; for it was at that
hour that Burrham was to distribute the cyclopædias at
Castle Garden. The Emigrant Commission had not yet
seized it for their own. I spent the morning in asking
vainly for Masons fresh from Europe, and for work in
cabinet-shops. I found neither, and so wrought my way
to the appointed place, where, instead of such wretched
birds in the bush, I was to get one so contemptible in
my hand.

Those who remember Jenny Lind's first triumph night
at Castle Garden have some idea of the crowd as it filled
gallery and floor of that immense hall when I entered.
I had given no thought to the machinery of this folly.
I only know that my ticket bade me be there at two
P. M. this day. But as I drew near, the throng, the
bands of policemen, the long queues of persons entering,
reminded me that here was an affair of ten thousand persons, and also that Mr. Burrham was not unwilling to
make it as showy, perhaps as noisy, an affair as was
respectable, by way of advertising future excursions and
distributions. I was led to seat No. 3,671 with a good
deal of parade, and when I came there I found I was
very much of a prisoner. I was late, or rather on the
stroke of two. Immediately, almost, Mr. Burrham arose
in the front and made a long speech about his liberality,
and the public's liberality, and everybody's liberality in

general, and the method of the distribution in particular.
The mayor and four or five other well-known and respectable gentlemen were kind enough to be present to
guarantee the fairness of the arrangements. At the suggestion of the mayor and the police, the doors would now
be closed, that no persons might interrupt the ceremony
till it was ended. And the distribution of the cyclopædias would at once go forward, in the order in which the
lots were drawn, — earliest numbers securing the earliest
impressions; which, as Mr. Burrham almost regretted to
say, were a little better than the latest. After these had
been distributed two figures would be drawn, — one
green and one red, to indicate the fortunate lady and
gentleman who would receive respectively the profits
which had arisen from this method of selling the cyclopædias, after the expenses of printing and distribution
had been covered, and after the magazines had been
ordered.

Great cheering followed this announcement from all
but me. Here I had shut myself up in this humbug
hall, for Heaven knew how long, on the most important
day of my life. I would have given up willingly my
cyclopædia and my chance at the " profits," for the certainty of seeing Fausta at five o'clock. If I did not see
her then, what might befall her, and when might I see
her again? An hour before this certainty was my own;
now it was only mine by my liberating myself from this
prison. Still I was encouraged by seeing that everything was conducted like clock-work. From literally a
hundred stations they were distributing the books. We
formed ourselves into queues as we pleased, drew our

numbers, and then presented ourselves at the bureaux, ordered our magazines, and took our cyclopædias. It would be done, at that rate, by half past four. An omnibus might bring me to the Park, and a Bowery car do the rest in time. After a vain discussion for the right of exit with one or two of the attendants, I abandoned myself to this hope, and began studying my cyclopædia.

It was sufficiently amusing to see ten thousand people resign themselves to the same task, and affect to be unconcerned about the green and red figures which were to divide the "profits." I tried to make out who were as anxious to get out of that tawdry den as I was. Four o'clock struck, and the distribution was not done. I began to be very impatient. What if Fausta fell into trouble? I knew, or hoped I knew, that she would struggle to the Astor Library, as to her only place of rescue and refuge, — her asylum. What if I failed her there? I who had pretended to be her protector! "Protector, indeed!" she would say, if she knew I was at a theatre witnessing the greatest folly of the age. And if I did not meet her to-day, when should I meet her? If she found her aunt, how should I find her? If she did not find her, — good God! that was worse, — where might she not be before twelve hours were over? Then the fatal trunk! I had told the police agent he might send it to the St. Nicholas, because I had to give him some address. But Fausta did not know this, and the St. Nicholas people knew nothing of us. I grew more and more excited, and when at last my next neighbor told me that it was half past four, I rose and insisted on leaving my seat. Two ushers with blue sashes almost held me down; they showed me the whole assembly sinking into quiet. In fact, at that moment Mr. Burrham was begging every one to be seated. I would not be seated. I would go to the door. I would go out. "Go, if you please!" said the usher next it, contemptuously. And I looked, and there was no handle! Yet this was not a dream. It is the way they arrange the doors in halls where they choose to keep people in their places. I could have collared that grinning blue sash. I did tell him I would wring his precious neck for him, if he did not let me out. I said I would sue him for false imprisonment; I would have a writ of *habeas corpus*.

"*Habeas corpus* be d—d!" said the officer, with an irreverent disrespect to the palladium. "If you are not more civil, sir, I will call the police, of whom we have plenty. You say you want to go out; you are keeping everybody in."

And, in fact, at that moment the clear voice of the mayor was announcing that they would not go on until there was perfect quiet; and I felt that I was imprisoning all these people, not they me.

"Child of the Public," said my mourning genius, "are you better than other men?" So I sneaked back to seat No. 3,671, amid the contemptuous and reproachful looks and sneers of my more respectable neighbors, who had sat where they were told to do. We must be through in a moment, and perhaps Fausta would be late also. If only the Astor would keep open after sunset! How often have I wished that since, and for less reasons!

Silence thus restored, Mr. A——, the mayor, led forward his little daughter, blindfolded her, and bade her put her hand into a green box, from which she drew out a green ticket. He took it from her, and read, in his clear voice again, "No. 2,973!" By this time we all knew where the "two thousands" sat. Then "nine hundreds" were not far from the front, so that it was not far that that frightened girl, dressed all in black, and heavily veiled, had to walk, who answered to this call. Mr. A—— met her, helped her up the stair upon the stage, took from her her ticket, and read, "Jerusha Stillingfleet, of Yellow Springs, who, at her death, as it seems, transferred this right to the bearer."

The disappointed nine thousand nine hundred and ninety-nine joined in a rapturous cheer, each man and woman, to show that he or she was not disappointed. The bearer spoke with Mr. Burrham, in answer to his questions, and, with a good deal of ostentation, he opened a check-book, filled a check and passed it to her, she signing a receipt as she took it, and transferring to him her ticket. So far, in dumb show, all was well. What was more to my purpose, it was rapid, for we should have been done in five minutes more, but that some devil tempted some loafer in a gallery to cry, "Face! face!" Miss Stillingfleet's legatee was still heavily veiled.

In one horrid minute that whole amphitheatre, which seemed to me then more cruel than the Coliseum ever was, rang out with a cry of "Face, face!" I tried the counter-cry of "Shame! shame!" but I was in disgrace among my neighbors, and a counter-cry never takes as its prototype does, either. At first, on the stage, they affected not to hear or understand; then there was a courtly whisper between Mr. Burrham and the lady; but Mr. A——, the mayor, and the respectable gentlemen, instantly interfered. It was evident that she would not unveil, and that they were prepared to indorse her refusal. In a moment more she courtesied to the assembly; the mayor gave her his arm, and led her out through a side door.

O, the yell that rose up then! The whole assembly stood up, and, as if they had lost some vested right, hooted and shrieked, "Back! back! Face! face!" Mr. A—— returned, made as if he would speak, came forward to the very front, and got a moment's silence.

"It is not in the bond, gentlemen," said he. "The young lady is unwilling to unveil, and we must not compel her."

"Face! face!" was the only answer, and oranges from up stairs flew about his head and struck upon the table, — an omen only fearful from what it prophesied. Then there was such a row for five minutes as I hope I may never see or hear again. People kept their places, fortunately, under a vague impression that they should forfeit some magic rights if they left those numbered seats. But when, for a moment, a file of policemen appeared in the orchestra, a whole volley of cyclopædias fell like rain upon their chief, with a renewed cry of "Face! face!"

At this juncture, with a good deal of knowledge of popular feeling, Mr. A—— led forward his child again. Frightened to death the poor thing was, and crying; he tied his handkerchief round her eyes hastily, and took her to the red box. For a minute the house was hushed. A cry of "Down! down!" and every one took his place as the child gave the red ticket to her father. He read it as before, "No. 3,671!" I heard the words as if he did not speak them. All excited by the delay and the row, by the injustice to the stranger and the personal injustice of everybody to me, I did not know, for a dozen seconds, that every one was looking towards our side of the house, nor was it till my next neighbor with the watch said, "Go, you fool," that I was aware that 3,671 was I! Even then, as I stepped down the passage and up the steps, my only feeling was, that I should get out of this horrid trap, and possibly find Miss Jones lingering near the Astor, — not by any means that I was invited to take a check for $ 5,000.

There was not much cheering. Women never mean to cheer, of course. The men had cheered the green ticket, but they were mad with the red one. I gave up my ticket, signed my receipt, and took my check, shook hands with Mr. A—— and Mr. Burrham, and turned to bow to the mob, — for mob I must call it now. But the cheers died away. A few people tried to go out, perhaps, but there was nothing now to retain any in their seats as before, and the generality rose, pressed down the passages, and howled, "Face! face!" I thought for a moment that I ought to say something, but they would not hear me, and, after a moment's pause, my passion to depart overwhelmed me. I muttered some apology to the gentlemen, and left the stage by the stage-door.

I had forgotten that to Castle Garden there can be no back entrance. I came to door after door, which were

all locked. It was growing dark. Evidently the sun
was set, and I knew the library-door would be shut at
sunset. The passages were very obscure. All around
me rang this horrid yell of the mob, in which all that I
could discern was the cry, "Face, face!" At last, as I
groped round, I came to a practicable door. I entered
a room where the western sunset glare dazzled me. I
was not alone. The veiled lady in black was there.
But the instant she saw me she sprang towards me, flung
herself into my arms, and cried : —

"Felix, is it you? — you are indeed my protector!"

It was Miss Jones! It was Fausta! She was the
legatee of Miss Stillingfleet. My first thought was, "O,
if that beggarly usher had let me go! Will I ever, ever
think I have better rights than the Public again?"

I took her in my arms. I carried her to the sofa. I
could hardly speak for excitement. Then I did say that
I had been wild with terror; that I had feared I had lost
her, and lost her forever; that to have lost that inter-
view would have been worse to me than death; for
unless she knew that I loved her better than man ever
loved woman, I could not face a lonely night, and
another lonely day.

"My dear, dear child," I said, "you may think me
wild; but I must say this, — it has been pent up too
long."

"Say what you will," she said after a moment, in
which still I held her in my arms; she was trembling so
that she could not have sat upright alone, — " say what
you will, if only you do not tell me to spend another day
alone."

And I kissed her, and I kissed her, and I kissed her, and I said, "Never, darling, God helping me, till I die!"

How long we sat there I do not know. Neither of us spoke again. For one, I looked out on the sunset and the bay. We had but just time to rearrange ourselves in positions more independent, when Mr. A—— came in, this time in alarm, to say: —

"Miss Jones, we must get you out of this place, or we must hide you somewhere. I believe, before God, they will storm this passage, and pull the house about our ears."

He said this, not conscious, as he began, that I was there. At that moment, however, I felt as if I could have met a million men. I started forward and passed him, saying, "Let me speak to them." I rushed upon the stage, fairly pushing back two or three bullies who were already upon it. I sprang upon the table, kicking down the red box as I did so, so that the red tickets fell on the floor and on the people below. One stuck in an old man's spectacles in a way which made the people in the galleries laugh. A laugh is a great blessing at such a moment. Curiosity is another. Three loud words spoken like thunder do a good deal more. And after three words the house was hushed to hear me. I said: —

"Be fair to the girl. She has no father nor mother. She has no brother nor sister. She is alone in the world, with nobody to help her but the public — and me!"

The audacity of the speech brought out a cheer, and we should have come off in triumph, when some rowdy — the original "face" man, I suppose — said, —

" And who are you ? "

If the laugh went against me now I was lost, of
course. Fortunately I had no time to think. I said
without thinking, —

" I am the Child of the Public, and her betrothed
husband ! "

O heavens ! what a yell of laughter, of hurrahings, of
satisfaction with a *dénouement*, rang through the house,
and showed that all was well. Burrham caught the
moment, and started his band, this time successfully, —
I believe with " See the Conquering Hero." The doors,
of course, had been open long before. Well-disposed
people saw they need stay no longer ; ill-disposed people
dared not stay ; the blue-coated men with buttons saun-
tered on the stage in groups, and I suppose the worst
rowdies disappeared as they saw them. I had made my
single speech, and for the moment I was a hero.

I believe the mayor would have liked to kiss me.
Burrham almost did. They overwhelmed me with thanks
and congratulations. All these I received as well as I
could, — somehow I did not feel at all surprised, —
everything was as it should be. I scarcely thought of
leaving the stage myself, till, to my surprise, the mayor
asked me to go home with him to dinner.

Then I remembered that we were not to spend the
rest of our lives in Castle Garden. I blundered out
something about Miss Jones, that she had no escort
except me, and pressed into her room to find her. A
group of gentlemen was around her. Her veil was back
now. She was very pale, but very lovely. Have I said
that she was beautiful as heaven ? She was the queen of

the room, modestly and pleasantly receiving their felicita-
tions that the danger was over, and owning that she had
been very much frightened. "Until," she said, "my
friend, Mr. Carter, was fortunate enough to guess that I
was here. How he did it," she said, turning to me, "is
yet an utter mystery to me."

She did not know till then that it was I who had
shared with her the profits of the cyclopædias.

As soon as we could excuse ourselves, I asked some
one to order a carriage. I sent to the ticket-office for
my valise, and we rode to the St. Nicholas. I fairly
laughed as I gave the hackman at the hotel-door what
would have been my last dollar and a half only two hours
before. I entered Miss Jones's name and my own.
The clerk looked, and said inquiringly, —

"Is it Miss Jones's trunk which came this afternoon?"

I followed his finger to see the trunk on the marble
floor. Rowdy Rob had deserted it, having seen, perhaps, a detective when he reached Piermont. The trunk
had gone to Albany, had found no owner, and had returned by the day boat of that day.

Fausta went to her room, and I sent her supper after
her. One kiss and "Good night" was all that I got
from her then.

"In the morning," said she, "you shall explain."

It was not yet seven. I went to my own room and
dressed, and tendered myself at the mayor's just before
his gay party sat down to dine. I met, for the first time
in my life, men whose books I had read, and whose
speeches I had by heart, and women whom I have since

known to honor; and, in the midst of this brilliant group, so excited had Mr. A—— been in telling the strange story of the day, I was, for the hour, the lion.

I led Mrs. A—— to the table; I made her laugh very heartily by telling her of the usher's threats to me, and mine to him, and of the disgrace into which I fell among the three thousand six hundreds. I had never been at any such party before. But I found it was only rather simpler and more quiet than most parties I had seen, that its good breeding was exactly that of dear Betsy Myers.

As the party broke up, Mrs. A—— said to me, —

"Mr. Carter, I am sure you are tired, with all this excitement. You say you are a stranger here. Let me send round for your trunk to the St. Nicholas, and you shall spend the night here. I know I can make you a better bed than they."

I thought as much myself, and assented. In half an hour more I was in bed in Mrs. A——'s "best room."

"I shall not sleep better," said I to myself, "than I did last night."

That was what the Public did for me that night. I was safe again!

III.

FAUSTA'S STORY.

FAUSTA slept late, poor child. I called for her before breakfast. I waited for her after. About ten she appeared, so radiant, so beautiful, and so kind! The trunk had revealed a dress I never saw before, and the sense of rest, and eternal security, and unbroken love had revealed a charm which was never there to see before. She was dressed for walking, and, as she met me, said, —

"Time for constitutional, Mr. Millionnaire."

So we walked again, quite up town, almost to the region of pig-pens and cabbage-gardens which is now the Central Park. And after just the first gush of my enthusiasm, Fausta said, very seriously : —

"I must teach you to be grave. You do not know whom you ~~ ~~~~~~ to be your wife. Excepting Mrs. Mason, No. 27 Thirty-fourth Street, sir, there is no one in the world who is of kin to me, and she does not care for me one straw, Felix," she said, almost sadly now. "You call yourself ' Child of the Public.' I started when you first said so, for that is just what I am.

"I am twenty-two years old. My father died before I was born. My mother, a poor woman, disliked by his relatives and avoided by them, went to live in Hoboken over there, with me. How she lived, God knows ! but it happened that of a strange death she died, I in her arms."

After a pause, the poor girl went on :

"There was a great military review, an encampment. She was tempted out to see it. Of a sudden, by some mistake, a ramrod was fired from a careless soldier's gun, and it pierced her through the heart. I tell you, Felix, it pinned my baby frock into the wound, so that they could not part me from her till it was cut away.

"Of course every one was filled with horror. Nobody claimed poor me, the baby. But the battalion — the

Montgomery Battalion, it was, which had, by mischance, killed my mother — adopted me as their child. I was voted 'Fille du Regiment.' They paid an assessment annually, which the colonel expended for me. A kind old woman nursed me."

"She was your Betsy Myers," interrupted I.

"And when I was old enough I was sent into Connecticut, to the best of schools. This lasted till I was sixteen. Fortunately for me, perhaps, the Montgomery Battalion then dissolved. I was finding it hard to answer the colonel's annual letters. I had my living to earn, — it was best I should earn it. I declined a proposal to go out as a missionary. I had no call. I answered one of Miss Beecher's appeals for Western teachers. Most of my life since has been a school-ma'am's. It has had ups and downs. But I have always been proud that the Public was my godfather; and, as you know," she said, "I have trusted the Public well. I have never been lonely, wherever I went. I tried to make myself of use. Where I was of use I found society. The ministers have been kind to me. I always offered my services in the Sunday schools and sewing-rooms. The school committees have been kind to me. They are the Public's high chamberlains for poor girls. I have written for the journals. I won one of Sartain's hundred-dollar prizes — "

"And I another," interrupted I.

"When I was very poor, I won the first prize for an essay on bad boys."

"And I the second," answered I.

"I think I know one bad boy better than he knows

8 *   L

himself," said she.   But she went on.   " I watched with
this poor Miss Stillingfleet the night she died.   This
absurd ' distribution' had got hold of her, and she would
not be satisfied till she had transferred that strange
ticket, No. 2,973, to me, writing the indorsement which
you have heard.   I had had a longing to visit New
York and Hoboken again.   This ticket seemed to me to
beckon me.   I had money enough to come, if I would
come cheaply.   I wrote to my father's business partner,
and enclosed a note to his only sister.   She is Mrs.
Mason.   She asked me, coldly enough, to her house.
Old Mr. Grills always liked me, — he offered me escort
and passage as far as Troy or Albany.   I accepted his
proposal, and you know the rest."

When I told Fausta my story, she declared I made
it up as I went along.   When she believed it, — as she
does believe it now, — she agreed with me in declaring
that it was not fit that two people thus joined should
ever be parted.   Nor have we been, ever!

She made a hurried visit at Mrs. Mason's.   She prepared there for her wedding.   On the 1st of November
we went into that same church which was our first home
in New York; and that dear old raven-man made us
one.

THE RIVAL DREAMERS.

BY JOHN BANIM.

R. WASHINGTON IRVING has already given
to the public a version of an American legend,
which, in a principal feature, bears some likeness to the following transcript of a popular Irish one.
It may, however, be interesting to show this very coincidence between the descendants of a Dutch transatlantic
colony and the native peasantry of Ireland, in the superstitious annals of both. Our tale, moreover, will be
found original in all its circumstances, that alluded to
only excepted.

Shamus Dempsey returned a silent, plodding, sorrowful
man, though a young one, to his poor home, after seeing
laid in the grave his aged, decrepit father. The last rays
of the setting sun were glorious, shooting through the
folds of their pavilion of scarlet clouds ; the last song of
the thrush, chanted from the bough nearest to his nest,
was gladdening ; the abundant though but half-matured
crops around breathed of hope for the future. But
Shamus's bosom was covered with the darkness that
inward sunshine alone can illumine. The chord that

should respond to song and melody had snapped in it;
for him the softly undulating fields of light-green wheat,
or the silken surfaced patches of barley, made a promise
in vain. He was poor, penniless, friendless, and yet
groaning under responsibilities : worn out by past and
present suffering, and without a consoling prospect.
His father's corpse had been just buried by a subscrip-
tion among his neighbors, collected in an old glove, a
penny or a half-penny from each, by the most active of
the humble community to whom his sad state was a
subject of pity. In the wretched shed which he called
"home," a young wife lay on a truss of straw, listening
to the hungry cries of two little children, and awaiting
her hour to become the weeping mother of a third.
And the recollection that but for an act of domestic
treachery experienced by his father and himself, both
would have been comfortable and respectable in the
world, aggravated the bitterness of the feeling in which
Shamus contemplated this lot. He could himself faintly
call to mind a time of early childhood, when he lived
with his parents in a roomy house, eating and sleeping
and dressing well, and surrounded by servants and workmen ; he further remembered that a day of great affliction came, upon which strange and rude persons forced
their way into the house ; and, for some cause his infant
observation did not reach, father, servants, and workmen
(his mother had just died) were all turned out upon the
road, and doomed to seek the shelter of a mean roof.
But his father's discourse, since he gained the years of
manhood, supplied Shamus with an explanation of all
these circumstance, as follows : —

Old Dempsey had been the youngest son of a large farmer, who divided his lands between two elder children, and destined Shamus's father to the Church, sending him abroad for education, and, during its course, supplying him with liberal allowances. Upon the eve of ordination the young student returned home to visit his friends; was much noticed by neighboring small gentry of each religion; at the house of one of the opposite persuasion from his met a sister of the proprietor, who had a fortune in her own right; abandoned his clerical views for her smiles; eloped with her; married her privately; incurred thereby the irremovable hostility of his own family; but, after a short time, was received, along with his wife, by his generous brother-in-law, under whose guidance both became reputably settled in the house to which Shamus's early recollections pointed, and where, till he was about six years old, he passed indeed a happy childhood.

But, a little previous to this time, his mother's good brother died unmarried, and was succeeded by another of her brothers, who had unsuccessfully spent half his life as a lawyer in Dublin, and who, inheriting little of his predecessor's amiable character, soon showed himself a foe to her and her husband, professedly on account of her marriage with a Roman Catholic. He did not appear to their visit, shortly after his arrival in their neighborhood, and he never condescended to return it. The affliction experienced by his sensitive sister, from his conduct, entailed upon her a premature accouchement, in which, giving birth to a lifeless babe, she unexpectedly died. The event was matter of triumph rather than of sorrow to her unnatural brother. For, in the first place, totally unguarded against the sudden result, she had died intestate; in the next place, he discovered that her private marriage had been celebrated by a Roman Catholic priest, consequently could not, according to law, hold good; and again, could not give to her nominal husband any right to her property, upon which both had hitherto lived, and which was now the sole means of existence to Shamus's father.

The lawyer speedily set to work upon these points, and with little difficulty succeeded in supplying for Shamus's recollections a day of trouble, already noticed. In fact, his father and he, now without a shilling, took refuge in a distant cabin, where, by the sweat of his parent's brow, as a laborer in the fields, the ill-fated hero of this story was scantily fed and clothed, until maturer years enabled him to relieve the old man's hand of the spade and sickle, and in turn labor for their common wants.

Shamus, becoming a little prosperous in the world, rented a few acres adjacent to his cabin and — married. The increase of his fields did not quite keep pace with the increase of his cares, in the persons of new-comers, for whose well-being he was bound to provide. His ray of success in life soon became overclouded, by the calls of the landlord and the tithe-proctor. In truth, three years after his marriage, he received a notice which it were vain to oppose, to quit both his farm and his cabin, and leave his few articles of furniture behind.

At this juncture his father was bedridden, and his wife advanced in her third pregnancy. He put on his hat, walked to the door, fixed his eyes upon the ruins of an old abbey which stood on the slope of an opposite hill, and formed his plan for present measures. By the next evening he had constructed a wattled shed, covered with rushes and leaves, against a gable in the interior of the ruin. Clearing away the nettles and other rank weeds enclosed by his new house, he discovered a long slab on which was carved a cross and letters illegible to his eye ; this he made his hearthstone. To furnish the abode, he fetched two large stones, as seats for his wife and himself, shook straw in either corner, and laid in a bundle of twigs. Then he went to the cabin that was no longer his, sent on his wife and two children to the abbey, followed with his father on his back, and laid him upon one of the straw couches. Two days afterwards the old man was a corpse. From his pauper funeral we now see Shamus returning, and to such a home does he bend his heavy steps.

If to know that the enemy of his father and mother did not thrive on the spoils of his oppression could have yielded Shamus any consolation in his lot, he had long ago become aware of circumstances calculated to give this negative comfort. His maternal uncle enjoyed, indeed, his newly acquired property only a few years after it came into his possession. Partly on account of his cruelty to his relations, partly from a meanness and vulgarity of character, which soon displayed itself in his novel situation, and which, it was believed, had previously kept him in the lowest walks of his profession as a Dublin attorney, he found himself neglected and shunned by the gentry of his neighborhood. To grow richer than any one who thus insulted him, to blazon abroad reports of his wealth, and to watch opportunities of using it to their injury, became the means of revenge adopted by the *parvenu*. His legitimate income not promising a rapid accomplishment of this plan, he ventured, using precautions that seemingly set suspicion at defiance, to engage in smuggling adventures on a large scale, for which his proximity to the coast afforded a local opportunity. Notwithstanding all his pettifogging cleverness, the ex-attorney was detected, however, in his illegal traffic, and fined to an amount which swept away half his real property. Driven to desperation by the publicity of his failure, as well as by the failure itself, he tried another grand effort to retrieve his fortune; was again surprised by the revenue officers; in a personal struggle with them, at the head of his band, killed one of their body; immediately absconded from Ireland; for the last twenty years had not been authentically heard of; but, it was believed, lived under an assumed name in London, deriving an obscure existence from some mean pursuit, of which the very nature enabled him to gratify propensities to drunkenness and other vices, learned during his first career in life.

All this Shamus knew, though only from report, inasmuch as his uncle had exiled himself while he was yet a child, and without previously having become known to the eyes of the nephew he had so much injured. But if Shamus occasionally drew a bitter and almost savage gratification from the downfall of his inhuman persecutor, no recurrence to the past could alleviate the misery of his present situation. He passed under one of the capacious open arches of the old abbey, and then entered his squalid shed reared against its wall, his heart as shattered and as

trodden down as the ruins around him. No words of
greeting ensued between him and his equally hopeless
wife, as she sat on the straw of her bed, rocking to sleep,
with feeble and mournful cries, her youngest infant. He
silently lighted a fire of withered twigs on his ready-fur-
nished hearthstone; put to roast among their embers a
few potatoes which he had begged during the day; divided them between her and her crying children; and as
the moon, rising high in the heavens, warned him that
night asserted her full empire over the departed day, Shamus sank down upon the couch from which his father's
mortal remains had lately been borne, supperless himself,
and dinnerless, too, but not hungry; at least not conscious or recollecting that he was.

His wife and little ones soon slept soundly, but Shamus
lay for hours inaccessible to nature's claims for sleep as
well as for food. From where he lay he could see, through
the open front of his shed, out into the ruins abroad.
After much abstraction in his own thoughts, the silence,
the extent, and the peculiar desolation of the scene, almost
spiritualized by the magic effect of alternate moonshine
and darkness, of objects and of their parts, at last di-
verted his mind, though not to relieve it. He remembered
distinctly, for the first time, where he was,—an intruder
among the dwellings of the dead; he called to mind, too,
that the present was their hour for revealing themselves
among the remote loneliness and obscurity of their crum-
bling and intricate abode. As his eye fixed upon a distant
stream of cold light or of blank shadow, either the waver-
ing of some feathery herbage from the walls, or the flitting
of some night bird over the roofless aisle, made motion

which went and came during the instant of his alarmed
start, or else some disembodied sleeper around had chal-
lenged and evaded his vision so rapidly as to baffle even
the accompaniment of thought.   Shamus would, however,
recur, during these entrancing aberrations, to his more
real causes for terror; and he knew not, and to this day
cannot distinctly tell, whether he waked or slept, when
a new circumstance absorbed his attention.   The moon
struck fully, under his propped roof, upon the carved slab
he had appropriated as a hearthstone, and turning his eye
to the spot, he saw the semblance of a man advanced in
years, though not very old, standing motionless, and very
steadfastly regarding him; the still face of the figure shone
like marble in the nightbeam, without giving any idea of
the solidity of that material; the long and deep shadows
thrown by the forehead over the eyes left those unusually
expressive features vague and uncertain.   Upon the head
was a close-fitting black cap, the dress was a loose-sleeved,
plaited garment of white, descending to the ground, and
faced and otherwise checkered with black, and girded
round the loins; exactly the costume which Shamus had
often studied in a little framed and glazed print, hung up
in the sacristry of the humble chapel recently built in the
neighborhood of the ruin by a few descendants of the
great religious fraternity to whom, in its day of pride, the
abbey had belonged.   As he returned very inquisitively,
though, as he avers, not now in alarm, the fixed gaze of
his midnight visitor, a voice reached him, and he heard
these strange words: —

"Shamus Dempsey, go to London Bridge, and you will
be a rich man."

"How will that come about, your reverence?" cried Shamus, jumping up from the straw.

But the figure was gone; and stumbling among the black embers on the remarkable place where it had stood, he fell prostrate, experiencing a change of sensation and of observance of objects around, which might be explained by supposing a transition from a sleeping to a waking state of mind.

The rest of the night he slept little, thinking of the advice he had received, and of the mysterious personage who gave it. But he resolved to say nothing about his vision, particularly to his wife, lest, in her present state of health, the frightful story might distress her; and, as to his own conduct respecting it, he determined to be guided by the future, — in fact, he would wait to see if his counsellor came again. He did come again, appearing in the same spot at the same hour of the night, and wearing the same dress, though not the same expression of feature; for the shadowy brows now slightly frowned, and a little severity mingled with the former steadfastness of look.

"Shamus Dempsey, why have you not gone to London Bridge, and your wife so near the time when she will want what you are to get by going there? Remember, this is my second warning."

"Musha, your reverence, an' what am I to do on Lunnon Bridge?"

Again he rose to approach the figure; again it eluded him. Again a change occurred in the quality of the interest with which he regarded the admonition of his visitor. Again he passed a day of doubt as to the propriety

of undertaking what seemed to him little less than a journey to the world's end, without a penny in his pocket,
and upon the eve of his wife's accouchement, merely in
obedience to a recommendation which, according to his
creed, was not yet sufficiently strongly given, even were
it under any circumstances to be adopted. For Shamus
had often heard, and firmly believed, that a dream or a
vision, instructing one how to procure riches, ought to
be experienced three times before it became entitled to
attention.

He lay down, however, half hoping that his vision
might thus recommend itself to his notice. It did so.

"Shamus Dempsey," said the figure, looking more
angry than ever, "you have not yet gone to London
Bridge, although I hear your wife crying out to bid you
go. And, remember, this is my third warning."

"Why, then, tundher-an-ouns, your reverence, just
stop and tell me — "

Ere he could utter another word the holy visitant
disappeared, in a real passion at Shamus's qualified
curse; and at the same moment his confused senses
recognized the voice of his wife, sending up from her
straw pallet the cries that betoken a mother's distant
travail. Exchanging a few words with her, he hurried
away, professedly to call up, at her cabin window, an
old crone who sometimes attended the very poorest
women in Nance Dempsey's situation.

"Hurry to her, Noreen, acuishla, and do the best it's
the will of God to let you do. And tell her from me,
Noreen — " He stopped, drawing in his lip, and clutch-
ing his cudgel hard.

"Shamus, what ails you, avick?" asked old Noreen; "what ails you, to make the tears run down in the gray o' the morning?"

"Tell her from me," continued Shamus, "that it's from the bottom o' the heart I'll pray, morning and evening, and fresh and fasting, maybe, to give her a good time of it; and to show her a face on the poor child that's coming, likelier than the two that God sent afore it. And that I'll be thinking o' picturing it to my own mind, though I'll never see it far away."

"Musha, Shamus, what are you speaking of?"

"No matter, Noreen, only God be wid you, and wid her, and wid the weenocks; and tell her what I bid you. More-be-token, tell her that poor Shamus quits her in her throuble, with more love from the heart out than he had for her the first day we came together; and I'll come back to her at any rate, sooner or later, richer or poorer, or as bare as I went; and maybe not so bare either. But God only knows. The top o' the morning to you, Noreen, and don't let her want the mouthful o' praties while I'm on my thravels. For this," — added Shamus, as he bounded off, to the consternation of old Noreen, — "this is the very morning and the very minute that, if I mind the dhrame at all at all, I ought to mind it; ay, without ever turning back to get a look from her, that 'ud kill the heart in my body entirely."

Without much previous knowledge of the road he was to take, Shamus walked and begged his way along the coast to the town where he might hope to embark for England. Here, the captain of a merchantman agreed to let him work his passage to Bristol, whence he again walked and begged into London.

Without taking rest or food, Shamus proceeded to London Bridge, often put out of his course by wrong directions, and as often by forgetting and misconceiving true ones. It was with old London Bridge that Shamus had to do (not the old one last pulled down, but its more reverend predecessor), which, at that time, was lined at either side by quaintly fashioned houses, mostly occupied by shop-keepers, so that the space between presented, perhaps, the greatest thoroughfare then known in the Queen of Cities. And at about two o'clock in the afternoon, barefooted, ragged, fevered, and agitated, Shamus mingled with the turbid human stream, that roared and chafed over the, as restless and as evanescent, stream which buffeted the arches of old London Bridge. In a situation so novel to him, so much more extraordinary in the reality than his anticipation could have fancied, the poor and friendless stranger felt overwhelmed. A sense of forlornness, of insignificance, and of terror seized upon his faculties. From the stare, or the sneers, or the jostle of the iron-nerved crowd, he shrank with glances of wild timidity, and with a heart as wildly timid as were his looks. For some time he stood or staggered about, unable to collect his thoughts, or to bring to mind what was his business there. But when Shamus became able to refer to the motive of his pauper journey, from his native solitudes into the thick of such a scene, it was no wonder that the zeal of superstition totally subsided amid the astounding truths he witnessed. In fact, the bewildered simpleton now regarded his dream as the merest chimera. Hastily escaping from the thoroughfare, he sought out some wretched place of repose suited to his wretched condition, and there moaned himself asleep, in self-accusations at the thought of poor Nance at home, and in utter despair of all his future prospects.

At daybreak the next morning he awoke, a little less agitated, but still with no hope. He was able, however, to resolve upon the best course of conduct now left open to him ; and he arranged immediately to retrace his steps to Ireland, as soon as he should have begged sufficient alms to speed him a mile on the road. With this intent he hastily issued forth, preferring to challenge the notice of chance passengers, even at the early hour of dawn, than to venture again, in the middle of the day, among the dreaded crowds of the vast city. Very few, indeed, were the passers-by whom Shamus met during his straggling and stealthy walk through the streets, and those of a description little able or willing to afford a halfpenny to his humbled, whining suit, and to his spasmed lip and watery eye. In what direction he went Shamus did not know; but at last he found himself entering upon the scene of his yesterday's terror. Now, however, it presented nothing to renew its former impression. The shops at the sides of the bridge were closed, and the occasional stragglers of either sex who came along inspired Shamus, little as he knew of a great city, with aversion rather than with dread. In the quietness and security of his present position, Shamus was both courageous and weak enough again to summon up his dream.

"Come," he said, "since I *am* on Lunnon Bridge,
I 'll walk over every stone of it, and see what good that
will do."

He valiantly gained the far end. Here one house, of
all that stood upon the bridge, began to be opened; it
was a public house, and, by a sidelong glance as he
passed, Shamus thought that, in the person of a red-
cheeked, red-nosed, sunk-eyed, elderly man, who took
down the window-shutters, he recognized the proprietor.
This person looked at Shamus, in return, with peculiar
scrutiny. The wanderer liked neither his regards nor
the expression of his countenance, and quickened his
steps onward until he cleared the bridge.

"But I 'll walk it over at the other side, now," he
bethought, after allowing the publican time to finish
opening his house, and retire out of view.

But, repassing the house, the man still appeared, lean-
ing against his door-jamb, and as if waiting for Shamus's
return, whom, upon this second occasion, he eyed more
attentively than before.

"Sorrow 's in him," thought Shamus, "have I two
heads on me, that I 'm such a sight to him? But who
cares about his pair of ferret-eyes? I 'll thrudge down
the middle stone of it, at any rate! "

Accordingly he again walked towards the public house,
keeping the middle of the bridge.

"Good morrow, friend," said the publican, as Shamus
a third time passed his door.

"Sarvant kindly, sir," answered Shamus, respectfully
pulling down the brim of his hat, and increasing his
pace.

" while you lie here awhile, an' no one to help you, in the cool of the morning, I 'll just take a start of you on the road home, to lift the flag and get the threasure; and follow me if you dare! You know there 's good money bid for your head in Ireland, — so here goes. Yes, faith and wid this — *this* to help me on the way!" He snatched up a heavy purse which had fallen from his uncle's pocket in the struggle. "And sure, there 's neither hurt nor harm in getting back a little of a body's own from you. A bright good-morning, uncle dear!"

Shamus dragged his manacled relative into the shop, quickly shut to and locked the door, flung the key over the house into the Thames, and the next instant was running at headlong speed.

He was not so deficient in the calculations of common-sense as to think himself yet out of his uncle's power. It appeared, indeed, pretty certain, that neither for the violence done to his person, nor for the purse appropriated by his nephew, the outlawed murderer would raise a hue and cry after one who, aware of his identity, could deliver him up to the laws of his country. But Shamus felt certain that it would be a race between him and his uncle for the treasure that lay under the friar's tombstone. His simple nature supplied no stronger motive for a pursuit on the part of a man whose life now lay in the breath of his mouth. Full of his conviction, however, Shamus saw he had not a moment to lose until the roof of his shed in the old abbey again sheltered him. So, freely making use of his uncle's guineas, he purchased a strong horse in the outskirts of London, and to the surprise, if not under heavy suspicions of the vender, set off at a gallop upon the road by which he had the day before gained the great metropolis.

A ship was ready to sail at Bristol for Ireland; but, to Shamus's discomfiture, she waited for a wind. He got aboard, however, and in the darksome and squalid hold often knelt down and, with clasped hands and panting breast, petitioned Heaven for a favorable breeze. But from morning until evening the wind remained as he had found it, and Shamus despaired. His uncle, meantime, might have reached some other port, and embarked for their country. In the depth of his anguish he heard a brisk bustle upon deck, clambered up to investigate its cause, and found the ship's sails already half unfurled to a wind that promised to bear him to his native shores by the next morning. The last light of day yet lingered in the heavens: he glanced, now under way, to the quay of Bristol. A group who had been watching the departure of the vessel turned round to note the approach to them of a man who ran furiously towards the place where they stood, pointing after her, and evidently speaking with vehemence, although no words reached Shamus's ear. Neither was his eye sure of this person's features; but his heart read them distinctly. A boat shot from the quay; the man stood up in it, and its rowers made a signal.

Shamus stepped to the gangway, as if preparing to hurl his pursuer into the sea. The captain took a speaking-trumpet, and informing the boat that he could not stop an instant, advised her to wait for another merchantman, which would sail in an hour. And during and after his

speech his vessel ploughed cheerily on, making as much
way as she was adapted to accomplish.

Shamus's bosom felt lightened of its immediate terror,
but not freed of apprehension for the future. The ship
that was to sail in an hour haunted his thoughts : he did
not leave the deck, and, although the night proved very
dark, his anxious eyes were never turned from the English coast. Unusual fatigue and want of sleep now and
then overpowered him, and his senses swam in a wild
and snatching slumber; but from this he would start,
crying out and clinging to the cordage, as the feverish
dream of an instant presented him with the swelling can-
vas of a fast-sailing ship, which came, suddenly bursting
through the gloom of midnight, alongside of his own.
Morning dawned, really to unveil to him the object of
his fears following almost in the wake of her rival. He
glanced in the opposite direction, and beheld the shores
of Ireland; in another hour he jumped upon them ; but
his enemy's face watched him from the deck of the companion vessel, now not more than a few ropes' lengths
distant.

Shamus mounted a second good horse, and spurred
towards home. Often did he look back, but without
seeing any cause for increased alarm. As yet, however,
the road had been level and winding, and therefore could
not allow him to span much of it at a glance. After
noon it ascended a high and lengthened hill, surrounded
by wastes of bog. As he gained the summit of this hill,
and again looked back, a horseman appeared, sweeping to
its foot. Shamus galloped at full speed down the now
quickly falling road; then along its level continuation

for about a mile; and then up another eminence, more lengthened, though not so steep as the former; and from it still he looked back, and caught the figure of the horseman breaking over the line of the hill he had passed. For hours such was the character of the chase; until the road narrowed and began to wind amid an uncultivated and uninhabited mountain wilderness. Here Shamus's horse tripped and fell; the rider, little injured, assisted him to his legs, and, with lash and spur, re-urged him to pursue his course. The animal went forward in a last effort, and, for still another span of time, well befriended his rider. A rocky valley, through which both had been galloping, now opened at its farther end, presenting to Shamus's eye, in the distance, the sloping ground, and the ruin which, with its mouldering walls, encircled his poor home; and the setting sun streamed golden rays through the windows and rents of the old abbey.

The fugitive gave a weak cry of joy, and lashed his beast again. The cry seemed to be answered by a shout; and a second time, after a wild plunge, the horse fell, now throwing Shamus off with a force that left him stunned. And yet he heard the hoofs of another horse come thundering down the rocky way; and, while he made a faint effort to rise on his hands and look at his pursuer, the horse and horseman were very near, and the voice of his uncle cried, "Stand!" at the same time that the speaker fired a pistol, of which the ball struck a stone at Shamus's foot. The next moment his uncle, having left his saddle, stood over him, presenting a second pistol, and he spoke in a low but distinct voice.

"Spawn of a beggar! This is not merely for the

chance of riches given by our dreams, though it seems, in the teeth of all I ever thought, that the devil tells truth at last. No, nor it is not quite for the blow; but it *is* to close the lips that, with a single word, can kill me. You die, to let me live!"

"Help!" aspirated Shamus's heart, turning itself to Heaven; "help me but now, not for the sake of the goold either, but for the sake of them that will be left on the wild world without me; for them help me, great God!"

Hitherto his weakness and confusion had left him passive. Before his uncle spoke the last words, his silent prayer was offered, and Shamus had jumped upon his assailant. They struggled, and dragged each other down. Shamus felt the muzzle of the pistol at his breast; heard it snap, — but only snap; he seized and mastered it, and once more the uncle was at the mercy of his nephew. Shamus's hand was raised to deal a good blow; but he checked himself, and addressed the almost senseless ears of his captive.

"No; you're my mother's blood, and a son of hers will never draw it from your heart; but I can make sure of you again, — stop a bit."

He ran to his own prostrate horse, took off its bridle and its saddle-girth, and with both secured his uncle's limbs, beyond all possibility of the struggler being able to escape from their control.

"There," resumed Shamus, "lie there till we have time to send an ould friend to see you, that, I 'll go bail, will take good care of your four bones. And do you know where I'm going now? You tould me, on Lun-

9 *

non Bridge, that you knew *that*, at least," — pointing to the abbey, — " ay, and the quare ould hearthstone that 's to be found in it. And so, look at this, uncle, honey," —he vaulted upon his relative's horse, — " I 'm just goin' to lift it off o' the barrel-pot full of good ould goold, and you have only to cry halves, and you 'll get it, as sure as that the big divvle is in the town you came from."

Nance Dempsey was nursing her new-born babe, sitting up in her straw, and doing very well after her late illness, when old Noreen tottered in from the front of the ruin, to tell her that " the body they were just speaking about was driving up the hill mad, like as if 't was his own sperit in great throuble." And the listener had not recovered from her surprise, when Shamus ran into the shed, flung himself kneeling by her side, caught her in his arms, then seized her infant, covered it with kisses, and then, roughly throwing it in her lap, turned to the fireplace, raised one of the rocky seats lying near it, poised the ponderous mass over the hearthstone, and shivered into pieces, with one crash, that solid barrier between him and his visionary world of wealth.

" It 's cracked he is, out an' out, of a certainty," said Nance, looking terrified at her husband.

" Nothing else am I," shouted Shamus, after groping under the broken slab ; " an', for a token, get along with yourself out of this, owld gran ! "

He started up and seized her by the shoulder. Noreen remonstrated. He stooped for a stone ; she ran ; he pursued her to the arches of the ruin. She stopped halfway down the descent. He pelted her with clods to the bottom, and along a good piece of her road homewards; and then danced back into his wife's presence.

"Now, Nance," he cried, "now that we're by ourselves, what noise is this like!"

"And he took out han'fuls after han'fuls of the ould goold, afore her face, my dear," added the original narrator of this story.

"An' after the gaugers and their crony, Ould Nick, ran off wid the uncle of him, Nance and he, and the childer, lived together in their father's and mother's house; and if they didn't live and die happy, I wish that you and I may."

THE THREEFOLD DESTINY.

BY NATHANIEL HAWTHORNE.

IN the twilight of a summer eve, a tall, dark figure, over which long and remote travel had thrown an outlandish aspect, was entering a village, not in "Fairy Londe," but within our own familiar boundaries. The staff on which this traveller leaned had been his companion from the spot where it grew, in the jungles of Hindostan; the hat, that overshadowed his sombre brow, had shielded him from the suns of Spain, but his cheek had been blackened by the red-hot wind of an Arabian desert, and had felt the frozen breath of an Arctic region. Long sojourning amid wild and dangerous men, he still wore beneath his vest the ataghan which he had once struck into the throat of a Turkish robber. In every foreign clime he had lost something of his New England characteristics; and, perhaps, from every people he had unconsciously borrowed a new peculiarity; so that when the world-wanderer again trod the street of his native village, it is no wonder that he passed unrecognized, though exciting the gaze and curiosity of all. Yet, as his arm casually touched that of a young woman, who was wending her way to an evening lecture, she started, and almost uttered a cry.

"Ralph Cranfield!" was the name that she half articulated.

"Can that be my old playmate, Faith Egerton?" thought the traveller, looking round at her figure, but without pausing.

Ralph Cranfield, from his youth upward, had felt himself marked out for a high destiny. He had imbibed the idea, — we say not whether it were revealed to him by witchcraft, or in a dream of prophecy, or that his brooding fancy had palmed its own dictates upon him as the oracles of a Sibyl, — but he had imbibed the idea, and held it firmest among his articles of faith, that three marvellous events of his life were to be confirmed to him by three signs.

The first of these three fatalities, and perhaps the one on which his youthful imagination had dwelt most fondly, was the discovery of the maid, who alone, of all the maids on earth, could make him happy by her love. He was to roam around the world till he should meet a beautiful woman, wearing on her bosom a jewel in the shape of a heart; whether of pearl, or ruby, or emerald, or carbuncle, or a changeful opal, or perhaps a priceless diamond, Ralph Cranfield little cared, so long as it were a heart of one peculiar shape. On encountering this lovely stranger, he was bound to address her thus: — "Maiden, I have brought you a heavy heart. May I rest its weight on you?" And if she were his fated bride, — if their kindred souls were destined to form a union here below, which all eternity should only bind more closely, — she would reply, with her finger on the heart-shaped jewel, " This token, which I have worn so long, is the assurance that you may ! "

And, secondly, Ralph Cranfield had a firm belief that there was a mighty treasure hidden somewhere in the earth, of which the burial-place would be revealed to none but him. When his feet should press upon the mysterious spot, there would be a hand before him, pointing downward, — whether carved of marble, or hewn in gigantic dimensions on the side of a rocky precipice, or perchance a hand of flame in empty air, he could not tell; but, at least, he would discern a hand, the fore-finger pointing downward, and beneath it the Latin word EFFODE, — Dig ! And digging thereabouts, the gold in coin or ingots, the precious stones, or of whatever else the treasure might consist, would be certain to reward his toil.

The third and last of the miraculous events in the life of this high-destined man was to be the attainment of extensive influence and sway over his fellow-creatures. Whether he were to be a king, and founder of an hered-itary throne, or the victorious leader of a people con-tending for their freedom, or the apostle of a purified and regenerated faith, was left for futurity to show. As messengers of the sign, by which Ralph Cranfield might recognize the summons, three venerable men were to claim audience of him. The chief among them, a digni-fied and majestic person, arrayed, it may be supposed, in the flowing garments of an ancient sage, would be the bearer of a wand, or prophet's rod. With this wand, or rod, or staff, the venerable sage would trace a certain figure in the air, and then proceed to make known his heaven-instructed message; which, if obeyed, must lead to glorious results.

With this proud fate before him, in the flush of his imaginative youth, Ralph Cranfield had set forth to seek the maid, the treasure, and the venerable sage with his gift of extended empire. And had he found them? Alas! it was not with the aspect of a triumphant man, who had achieved a nobler destiny than all his fellows, but rather with the gloom of one struggling against peculiar and continual adversity, that he now passed homeward to his mother's cottage. He had come back, but only for a time, to lay aside the pilgrim's staff, trusting that his weary manhood would regain somewhat of the elasticity of youth, in the spot where his threefold fate had been foreshown him. There had been few changes in the village; for it was not one of those thriving places where a year's prosperity makes more than the havoc of a century's decay; but like a gray hair in a young man's head, an antiquated little town, full of old maids, and aged elms, and moss-grown dwellings. Few seemed to be the changes here. The drooping elms, indeed, had a more majestic spread; the weather-blackened houses were adorned with a denser thatch of verdant moss; and doubtless there were a few more gravestones in the burial-ground, inscribed with names that had once been familiar in the village street. Yet, summing up all the mischief that ten years had wrought, it seemed scarcely more than if Ralph Cranfield had gone forth that very morning, and dreamed a daydream till the twilight, and then turned back again. But his heart grew cold, because the village did not remember him as he remembered the village.

"Here is the change!" sighed he, striking his hand upon his breast. "Who is this man of thought and care, weary with world wandering, and heavy with disappointed hopes? The youth returns not, who went forth so joyously!"

And now Ralph Cranfield was at his mother's gate, in front of the small house where the old lady, with slender but sufficient means, had kept herself comfortable during her son's long absence. Admitting himself within the enclosure, he leaned against a great old tree, trifling with his own impatience, as people often do in those intervals when years are summed into a moment. He took a minute survey of the dwelling, — its windows, brightened with the sky gleam, its doorway, with the half of a millstone for a step, and the faintly traced path waving thence to the gate. He made friends again with his childhood's friend, the old tree against which he leaned; and glancing his eye adown its trunk, beheld something that excited a melancholy smile. It was a half-obliterated inscription, — the Latin word EFFODE, — which he remembered to have carved in the bark of the tree, with a whole day's toil, when he had first begun to muse about his exalted destiny. It might be accounted a rather singular coincidence, that the bark, just above the inscription, had put forth an excrescence, shaped not unlike a hand, with the forefinger pointing obliquely at the word of fate. Such, at least, was its appearance in the dusky light.

"Now a credulous man," said Ralph Cranfield care-

lessly to himself, "might suppose that the treasure which
I have sought round the world lies buried, after all, at
the very door of my mother's dwelling. That would be
a jest indeed! "

More he thought not about the matter; for now the
door was opened, and an elderly woman appeared on the
threshold, peering into the dusk to discover who it might
be that had intruded on her premises, and was standing
in the shadow of her tree. It was Ralph Cranfield's
mother. Pass we over their greeting, and leave the one to
her joy and the other to his rest, — if quiet rest be found.

But when morning broke, he arose with a troubled
brow; for his sleep and his wakefulness had alike been
full of dreams. All the fervor was rekindled with which
he had burned of yore to unravel the threefold mystery
of his fate. The crowd of his early visions seemed to
have awaited him beneath his mother's roof, and thronged
riotously around to welcome his return. In the well-
remembered chamber — on the pillow where his infancy
had slumbered — he had passed a wilder night than ever
in an Arab tent, or when he had reposed his head in the
ghastly shades of a haunted forest. A shadowy maid
had stolen to his bedside, and laid her finger on the scin-
tillating heart; a hand of flame had glowed amid the
darkness, pointing downward to a mystery within the
earth; a hoary sage had waved his prophetic wand, and
beckoned the dreamer onward to a chair of state. The
same phantoms, though fainter in the daylight, still
flitted about the cottage, and mingled among the crowd
of familiar faces that were drawn thither by the news of
Ralph Cranfield's return, to bid him welcome for his

N

mother's sake. There they found him, a tall, dark, stately man, of foreign aspect, courteous in demeanor and mild of speech, yet with an abstracted eye, which seemed often to snatch a glance at the invisible.

Meantime the widow Cranfield went bustling about the house, full of joy that she again had somebody to love, and be careful of, and for whom she might vex and tease herself with the petty troubles of daily life. It was nearly noon, when she looked forth from the door, and descried three personages of note coming along the street, through the hot sunshine and the masses of elm-tree shade. At length they reached her gate, and undid the latch.

"See, Ralph!" exclaimed she, with maternal pride, "here is Squire Hawkwood and the two other selectmen, coming on purpose to see you! Now do tell them a good long story about what you have seen in foreign parts."

The foremost of the three visitors, Squire Hawkwood, was a very pompous, but excellent old gentleman, the head and prime mover in all the affairs of the village, and universally acknowledged to be one of the sagest men on earth. He wore, according to a fashion even then becoming antiquated, a three-cornered hat, and carried a silver-headed cane, the use of which seemed to be rather for flourishing in the air than for assisting the progress of his legs. His two companions were elderly and respectable yeomen, who, retaining an ante-revolutionary reverence for rank and hereditary wealth, kept a little in the Squire's rear. As they approached along the pathway, Ralph Cranfield sat in an oaken elbow-chair, half unconsciously gazing at the three visitors, and

enveloping their homely figures in the misty romance
that pervaded his mental world.

"Here," thought he, smiling at the conceit, — "here
come three elderly personages, and the first of the three
is a venerable sage with a staff. What if this embassy
should bring me the message of my fate!"

While Squire Hawkwood and his colleagues entered,
Ralph rose from his seat, and advanced a few steps to
receive them; and his stately figure and dark countenance, as he bent courteously towards his guests, had a
natural dignity; contrasting well with the bustling importance of the Squire. The old gentleman, according
to invariable custom, gave an elaborate preliminary flourish with his cane in the air, then removed his three-
cornered hat in order to wipe his brow, and finally
proceeded to make known his errand.

"My colleagues and myself," began the Squire, "are
burdened with momentous duties, being jointly selectmen of this village. Our minds, for the space f three
days past, have been laboriously bent on the selectio. of
a suitable person to fill a most important office, and take
upon himself a charge and rule, which, wisely considered,
may be ranked no lower than those of kings and potentates. And whereas you, our native townsman, are of
good natural intellect, and well cultivated by foreign
travel, and that certain vagaries and fantasies of your
youth are doubtless long ago corrected, — taking all these
matters, I say, into due consideration, we are of opinion
that Providence hath sent you hither, at this juncture,
for our very purpose."

During this harangue, Cranfield gazed fixedly at the

speaker, as if he beheld something mysterious and unearthly in his pompous little figure, and as if the Squire had worn the flowing robes of an ancient sage, instead of a square-skirted coat, flapped waistcoat, velvet breeches, and silk stockings. Nor was his wonder without sufficient cause; for the flourish of the Squire's staff, marvellous to relate, had described precisely the signal in the air which was to ratify the message of the prophetic Sage, whom Cranfield had sought around the world.

"And what," inquired Ralph Cranfield, with a tremor in his voice, — "what may this office be, which is to equal me with kings and potentates?"

"No less than instructor of our village school," answered Squire Hawkwood; "the office being now vacant by the death of the venerable Master Whitaker, after a fifty years' incumbency."

"I will consider of your proposal," replied Ralph Cranfield, hurriedly, "and will make known my decision within three days."

After a few more words, the village dignitary and his companions took their leave. But to Cranfield's fancy their images were still present, and became more and more invested with the dim awfulness of figures which had first appeared to him in a dream, and afterwards had shown themselves in his waking moments, assuming homely aspects among familiar things. His mind dwelt upon the features of the Squire, till they grew confused with those of the visionary Sage, and one appeared but the shadow of the other. The same visage, he now thought, had looked forth upon him from the Pyramid of Cheops; the same form had beckoned to him among the colonnades of the Alhambra; the same figure had mistily revealed itself through the ascending steam of the Great Geyser. At every effort of his memory he recognized some trait of the dreamy Messenger of Destiny, in this pompous, bustling, self-important, little great man of the village. Amid such musings, Ralph Cranfield sat all day in the cottage, scarcely hearing and vaguely answering his mother's thousand questions about his travels and adventures. At sunset he roused himself to take a stroll, and, passing the aged elm-tree, his eye was again caught by the semblance of a hand, pointing downward at the half-obliterated inscription.

As Cranfield walked down the street of the village, the level sunbeams threw his shadow far before him; and he fancied that, as his shadow walked among distant objects, so had there been a presentiment stalking in advance of him throughout his life. And when he drew near each object, over which his tall shadow had preceded him, still it proved to be one of the familiar recollections of his infancy and youth. Every crook in the pathway was remembered. Even the more transitory characteristics of the scene were the same as in bygone days. A company of cows were grazing on the grassy roadside, and refreshed him with their fragrant breath. "It is sweeter," thought he, "than the perfume which was wafted to our ship from the Spice Islands. The round little figure of a child rolled from a doorway, and lay laughing almost beneath Cranfield's feet. The dark and stately man stooped down, and, lifting the infant, restored him to his mother's arms. "The children," said he to himself, — and sighed, and

smiled, — "the children are to be my charge!" And
while a flow of natural feeling gushed like a wellspring
in his heart, he came to a dwelling which he could nowise forbear to enter. A sweet voice, which seemed to
come from a deep and tender soul, was warbling a
plaintive little air, within.

He bent his head, and passed through the lowly door.
As his foot sounded upon the threshold, a young woman
advanced from the dusky interior of the house, at first
hastily, and then with a more uncertain step, till they
met face to face. There was a singular contrast in their
two figures; he dark and picturesque,— one who had bat-
tled with the world,— whom all suns had shone upon, and
whom all winds had blown on a varied course; she neat,
comely, and quiet,— quiet even in her agitation,— as if
all her emotions had been subdued to the peaceful tenor
of her life. Yet their faces, all unlike as they were, had
an expression that seemed not so alien,— a glow of kindred feeling, flashing upward anew from half-extinguished
embers.

"You are welcome home!" said Faith Egerton.

But Cranfield did not immediately answer; for his eye
had been caught by an ornament in the shape of a Heart,
which Faith wore as a brooch upon her bosom. The material was the ordinary white quartz; and he recollected
having himself shaped it out of one of those Indian arrow-
heads, which are so often found in the ancient haunts of
the red men. It was precisely on the pattern of that worn
by the visionary Maid. When Cranfield departed on his
shadowy search he had bestowed this brooch, in a gold
setting, as a parting gift to Faith Egerton.

"So, Faith, you have kept the Heart!" said he, at length.

"Yes," said she, blushing deeply; then, more gayly, "and what else have you brought me from beyond the sea?"

"Faith!" replied Ralph Cranfield, uttering the fated words by an uncontrollable impulse, "I have brought you nothing but a heavy heart! May I rest its weight on you?"

"This token, which I have worn so long," said Faith, laying her tremulous finger on the Heart, "is the assurance that you may!"

"Faith! Faith!" cried Cranfield, clasping her in his arms, "you have interpreted my wild and weary dream!"

Yes, the wild dreamer was awake at last. To find the mysterious treasure, he was to till the earth around his mother's dwelling, and reap its products! Instead of warlike command, or regal or religious sway, he was to rule over the village children! And now the visionary Maid had faded from his fancy, and in her place he saw the playmate of his childhood! Would all, who cherish such wild wishes, but look around them, they would oftenest find their sphere of duty, of prosperity, and happiness, within those precincts, and in that station, where Providence itself has cast their lot. Happy they who read the riddle, without a weary world-search, or a lifetime spent in vain!